one moment

KRISTINA
McBRIDE

one moment

EGMONT
USA
New York

EGMONT

We bring stories to life

First published by Egmont USA, 2012
443 Park Avenue South, Suite 806
New York, NY 10016

1 3 5 7 9 8 6 4 2

www.egmontusa.com

Library of Congress Cataloging-in-Publication Data

McBride, Kristina.
One moment / Kristina McBride.
p.   cm.
Summary: Rising high school senior Maggie remembers little about the
accidental death of her boyfriend, Joey, but as she slowly begins to recall
that day at the gorge with their long-time friends, she realizes he was
keeping some terrible secrets.
ISBN 978-1-60684-086-3 (hardcover) — ISBN 978-1-60684-269-0
(ebook) [1. Secrets—Fiction. 2. Friendship—Fiction. 3. Dating
(Social customs)—Fiction. 4. Amnesia—Fiction. 5. Death—Fiction.
6. Family life—Ohio—Fiction. 7. Ohio—Fiction.] I. Title.
PZ7.M1223One 2012
[Fic]—dc23
2011034335

Printed in the United States of America

To my parents,
who have spent many moments
listening to, supporting,
encouraging, and loving me.

contents

1

So Close to Flying

"So you're gonna do it?" Adam looked at me, his sun-blazed cheeks aglow with a daring smile.

I was sitting on Joey's damp towel near the lower bank of the gorge, squinting at the large rock wall fifty feet away, my hands propped behind me on a cool patch of grassy ground. Light sparkled off the rippling water swirling in a deep pool before us, flashing me a warning I would never decode. Joey was there, tangled in the message, floating on his back and squirting water up from his mouth like he was some lazy fountain.

"I said I'd do it." My eyes trailed up the wall, stopping at a tangle of trees and vines. Bright patches of azure sky peeked through fluttering leaves, like a child searching for a long-lost promise. My head was heavy from the beer I'd drunk, the heat of the sun, and the twang of Kid Rock's "All Summer Long" coming from the iPod dock beside me. My body practically screamed with the twining fear that had curled itself into every space within me.

"You sure?" Adam playfully swiped my damp bangs into my face.

"No freaking way she's gonna do it," Shannon said. She was lying on a fuzzy yellow towel, lazily running her fingers through her thick tangled brown waves, her sunglasses propped on the bridge of her nose.

"Maggie's full of surprises." Tanna stood from her towel and drifted toward the edge of the water. Her long blond hair, tied loosely in two braids, fell forward as she turned. "Isn't she, Joey?"

"What's that?" he asked, standing. I imagined mud squishing through his toes.

"Maggie." Tanna smiled, scrunching up her tiny nose. "She's a wild one."

Joey laughed. "My Maggie?"

"She's gonna do it this time." Adam offered me a hand and pulled me up. "You'll love it. Total free fall. It's like you're flying."

"Last time all she did was stand up there and hyperventilate," said Shannon. "You don't have to do it, Mags. We'll love you anyway."

"Of course we will." Joey stumbled as he made his way up the bank, water dripping off his tanned skin with bright sparkles. "But if you jump, we'll think you're a rock star."

Tanna laughed. "Maggie's already a rock star."

"I know exactly what Joey's thinking," Shannon said. "If she jumps off the cliff, he might finally get her to jump into his bed."

"Shannon!" I leaned down and smacked her bare thigh,

dying to tell both Shannon and Tanna to shut up before they ruined the plan I'd been working on for weeks.

"What?" Shannon asked, sitting up and adjusting the strap of her bikini top. "It's not like we don't all know that you two haven't sealed the deal."

"You have nothing to be ashamed of." Tanna twirled one of her braids between two fingers.

"Of course not." Shannon tipped her head back, turning her face to the sun. "I'm just being honest is all."

"Because you're always so honest?" Joey snorted.

Shannon didn't respond. Just whipped her hair from one shoulder to the other like she couldn't care less what anyone thought of her.

Joey rolled his eyes, then looked toward me with a wide grin. I tried to focus on the shimmering droplets of water falling from his longish brown hair, instead of the ball of panic that was coming to life in my chest. But it was difficult.

"Ready?" he asked, reaching his hand out and snagging my arm in his. It felt nice, his warm skin sliding against mine.

I nodded, unable to speak. I wasn't sure if I would ever be ready. But I knew I had to do it.

"Clear?" A deep voice echoed off the walls of the gorge, tumbling down the rocks.

We all looked up, Joey and me, Tanna, Adam. Shannon, too, though it seemed as if she was focused on something beyond the cliff top, her eyes sparking in the rays of light cascading from the blue, blue sky.

"All clear." Adam cupped his hands around his mouth to shout the familiar go-ahead. "Jump on!"

3

Pete, who was standing at the edge of the cliff looking down, gave us a thumbs-up before turning away, his thick dreadlocks swaying with his head. He disappeared after only a few steps, the height and angle of the cliff hiding him from our view. And all we could do was wait.

I held my breath as I stood there, watching in silence as he flung himself out into open air, spun around a few times, and dropped through the plane of the water with a glittering splash.

When Pete surfaced, his laughter pinged around us in a crazy dance. That was one of the things I loved most about the gorge. The way it took sound and distorted it, flung it around like it was something tangible but as light as air.

"*That*," Pete shouted with a laugh, "is the best rush in the world."

"Maggie's going up," Shannon said. Her voice was tinged with vicious energy, making me more determined to follow through with the jump that had started out as a simple dare. Shannon had pulled the same thing the first time Tanna decided to jump. It was like she needed to be the only girl bold enough to take the thirty-foot plunge, but she'd just have to get over it.

Joey, Adam, and Pete had found the cliff one day during the summer before eighth grade. After a long upstream hike along the creek that bordered our sleepy nothing-ever-happens-here neighborhood in Blue Springs, Ohio, they came to the top of the cliff. Once Joey, the oldest of us all, had his driver's license, he'd found an easier route, starting with a parking lot and one-mile trail. I loved the gorge, especially our Jumping Hole, even if Shannon was acting bitchy. Besides, I had more important things to worry about. Like survival.

"Rock on," Pete said, pumping a fist in the air, flinging water everywhere.

"I'd prefer if you didn't use phrases that include the word *rock* right now, seeing as how my main goal in the next twenty minutes will be to *avoid* all rocks," I said, glaring at him.

"You'll be fine," Joey said, one hand rubbing my back, the other pointing to a spot halfway up the steep wall. Or halfway down, depending on how you viewed things. "All you have to do is miss that ledge and you're golden."

"Right." I twisted my hair up into a messy bun and secured it in place with a hair band. "Miss the ledge. Golden. Does that mean I can have a swig of that tequila once this is over?"

"You can have anything you'd like," Joey said, goosing my butt.

I squealed and jumped away from him, swatting at his hand. "Will you stop it? This is serious."

Joey shrugged. "Made you laugh, didn't I?"

"I'm too nervous to laugh." I attempted to smile, but I wasn't sure if it worked. "Let's just go."

Joey and I made our way down the trail, toward what we'd always called the Jumping Rocks, a natural bridge that crossed the creek and led to the cliff-top trail. I stumbled the first few steps but fell into pace beside him quickly, almost melting into his warm, reassuring body.

"It's no scarier than The Beast," Joey said. "That's your favorite roller coaster at King's Island, isn't it?"

5

"The Beast has a harness to strap me in. Doesn't compare."

The trail twisted to our right just downstream from the Jumping Hole, and Joey hopped across several boulders bridging the narrower section of water. When he reached the middle and largest rock, he stopped and held out his hand. I leaped toward him, crashing into his lean body, almost toppling him over.

We laughed and bowed our heads together. He kissed me lightly on the lips. "You can do it," he whispered, the tart smell of the beer he'd drunk invading me.

"Sometimes, when I'm with you, I feel like I can do just about anything." I almost told him that I loved him. It would have been the perfect moment. But whenever I thought about saying those three words, I remembered what Joey had said when we'd first started dating.

We'd been driving—to Shannon's for one of her infamous, my-parents-are-out-of-town-again parties—and I was talking about how, even though it's totally cliché, I'd had that butterfly feeling in my stomach while I was waiting for him to pick me up. He'd looked at me then, maybe sensing where I was headed after three months of dating, and said, "Can we make a deal?" I'd been a little nervous but nodded my head anyway. I remember the taste of my Razzy-Tazzy lip gloss, how it turned bitter with my fear of what he was about to say. "Let's never pull the *I Love You* card. It's like a curse. And I like you too much to let it ruin things." He'd actually held his hand out. I thought he'd wanted to hold mine for the rest of the ride, but when my palm met his, his fingers curled upward like a Venus flytrap, and he gave my hand three short shakes before letting go. "It's a deal," I'd said with one of the fakest smiles I'd ever worn.

That had been about a year and a half ago. I wondered if the statute of limitations on our deal had passed. But standing there on the rock with Joey, with the steady flow of water rushing toward us and then away, with the steep dirt trail calling to me, I did not have the focus to wonder such things for long. I could deal with that later. After the last day of school, when we would officially be seniors. After our first time, which I'd secretly planned for the first week of summer when his parents were heading out of town for an entire week.

I took a deep breath, tasting the honeysuckle that saturated the air around the rock bridge, and swallowed my words. He knew I loved him. I didn't need to say it.

My chest was heaving, my thighs screaming, but I pushed myself forward. I hadn't climbed the narrow dirt trail leading to the top of the cliff since the previous fall, when I'd chickened out of the jump and had to scurry back down again. The light-headed feeling I'd experienced that day was threatening to take over again, so I tried to focus on my feet, the steps, anything but the reason that I was steadily moving away from solid ground.

"You're lookin' pretty good from this angle," Joey said from behind me, swatting the butt of my black bikini bottoms. "Is it terrible that I'm hoping you lose your top on impact?"

"Joey, sometimes you border on pervert."

"I'm a seventeen-year-old guy. Whaddo you expect?"

I turned, propping my hands on my hips. "Let's switch places and see how you like being objectified." Waving a hand in the air, I indicated that he should take the lead.

"Oh, baby!" Joey held on to my shoulders as he passed, leaning in to nip at my neck with his teeth. That's when I noticed something different about him.

It was a bracelet. A small and totally insignificant accessory. But something about it bothered me.

I studied it as we climbed, the way the leather strap tied around his wrist slid up and down with the swing of his arm. The way the sun glistened off the three turquoise-colored glass beads threaded onto the leather.

"Where'd you get that?" I asked when we'd reached the flat part of the climb.

"Where'd I get what? My fine ass? My rippling muscles?"

"Your bracelet."

Joey swung his arm up, as if he'd forgotten he was even wearing a bracelet. He paused for a beat. "Found it in the laundry room. I thought it was cool, so I snagged it. Rylan's probably gonna be pissed."

Something was off, but I couldn't wrap my mind around it. And then I wasn't sure if my stomach had bottomed out because of Joey and that bracelet, or because I was standing at the top of the cliff looking down at my friends, getting ready to jump. A breeze stirred and I swayed with the treetops, the prickly feeling of terror spreading through my body.

8

"You can do it, Maggie," Tanna yelled up to me.

"Don't stand there looking down for too long," Adam called. "Just figure out how far right you need to be to avoid the ledge."

Shannon must have said something, because I saw Tanna smack her arm.

"What's her problem, anyway?" I asked, trying to focus on anything but the wide open space before me that was causing my vision to blur.

"Who?" Joey looked at me, his blue eyes eerily alive in the sunlight.

"Umm, Shannon," I said, like he was clueless. "She's being such a bitch."

"Isn't she kind of always a bitch?"

I shrugged.

"I thought that's part of what we all love about her." Joey wrapped his arm around my waist and pulled me to him. "Focus."

I nodded once, feeling a little dizzy.

"You can do this."

I nodded again, sure that the world was tumbling through space at super-warp speed with gravity pressing me forward and the universe itself daring me to leap over the edge of the cliff.

"I'm going to jump left, so you don't have to worry about the ledge."

"Can we hold hands?" I felt like a little kid, but I needed a connection to something real and stable if I was going to do this.

Joey smiled and bumped his nose against mine. "Of course."

"How far back do we have to go?"

Joey took ten or fifteen steps away from the edge of the cliff, turned, and held out his hand. "We just need to get a running start."

"Why does there need to be any running?"

"Momentum. We need to jump as far from the wall as we can."

"Oh. Duh."

I walked toward Joey and took his hand. He squeezed mine. I squeezed his in return. From where we stood, I could only see the edge of the cliff and a leafy batch of swaying treetops beyond. It was as if our friends didn't exist.

"We're gonna go on three," he said. "You ready?"

I shook my head. "No."

"You trust me?"

I looked at him then. Took in his freckled nose, the wisps of damp hair clinging to his forehead, the way his smile always tilted to the left.

I nodded. "I trust you."

He squeezed my hand again. "Everything's gonna be fine."

I ran my thumb up the inside of his wrist, feeling his blood, his life, pulsing through his body.

"One."

The cool shock of those turquoise beads zapped my skin like I'd been electrocuted.

"Two."

What was it about those beads?

"Three!"

Running.

We were running.

Almost there.

But the thunder of my feet crashed through something in my consciousness.

And I knew.

It was like I hit an invisible wall. One that did not exist for Joey.

I had been so close to flying.

Then, suddenly—I stopped.

2
The Ripple of My Fear

Screaming. Someone was screaming. Maybe more than one someone.

Or was that a trick?

The sound bouncing—bouncing—bouncing off the walls of the gorge.

I was on my knees. Sharp rocks biting into my bare skin. Little, prickly teeth.

What was going on?

I remembered climbing. Joey smacking my butt. But that was it.

Splashing. There was splashing, too.

And I remembered where I was.

At. The. Top.

But I wouldn't look.

Couldn't.

Then the screams broke open.

Turned into words.

One word—bouncing—bouncing—bouncing.

"No! No! No!"

And then I was running. Shades of green racing past me. Bright flashes of light.

Claws tearing at my legs, my arms, my face. Slicing me open.

Everything in my mind had flung itself into the air, splintered into a million tiny pieces, and rearranged itself into a jumbled mess.

I had to figure it out. Something. There was something I needed to understand. But I knew I didn't want to. Whatever it was—back there.

Hide.

I could hide.

There, in the underbrush of that tree. The slender sprouts creeping up from the ground leaning against it like a leafy tent.

Perfect.

I slid under the waxy shelter, pulling my knees to my chest. My breath coming in short bursts, exploding out of me.

Tipping my head back was bad. It made me dizzy.

But forward was worse.

That made me throw up. The sticky mess covered my right thigh. I didn't even bother to wipe it away.

There was something I had to understand.

I tried. Really I did. I'm not sure how much time passed as I sat there riffling through the disconnected bursts that whipped through my mind—one minute—or a million. And I couldn't figure it out. Didn't know if I would ever understand. Still, I kept trying. It was the only thing I could do.

But the footsteps interfered—heavy, clomping footsteps that made the earth vibrate beneath me.

I tried to hold my breath, to keep from shaking, so the ripple of my fear wouldn't strike the person coming down the trail, so they wouldn't know where I'd folded up and hidden myself.

It didn't work. He felt me. And he stopped.

"Maggie?" he was out of breath. Like me. Huffing and puffing, sucking in the air like there wasn't enough. "Maggie, I can see your feet."

Feet. I looked at my feet, at the Totally Teal polish I'd painted on my nails last night. Just last night. For the party.

"I—" I tried to speak, but my throat was crackle dry, on fire.

Adam leaned down, crawled toward me, and put his hand on my knee. I saw blood and didn't know if it was his or mine. "Are you hurt?"

Hurt?

I thought about that for a second. Shook my head.

Adam looked at me, the green of his eyes reminding me of sea glass. I could smell something rancid, and I wondered if it was me. Or him. Or something dead, rotting and seeping into the ground beneath us. Then I remembered I'd thrown up.

"Maggie," Adam said, his voice slow and cautious, "what happened?"

I closed my eyes. Squeezed them tight. And I tried to remember.

"Screaming," I said. "I heard screaming."

14   "Yeah." Adam ran a hand through his hair, tugging

plastered strands of golden blond away from his forehead. "I meant before the screaming. What happened before the screaming?"

"The music," I said. "Kid Rock. I remember singing 'All Summer Long' with Tanna and Shannon."

"Right. I remember that, too."

"And the Jumping Rocks. Standing on the rocks with Joey, the water all around. He kissed me." I smiled, practically feeling the flutter of his lips against mine. But when I opened my eyes, he wasn't there. It was Adam, his eyes wild, his lips pressed tight. "He kissed me."

Adam nodded. "What happened after that?" he asked. "After you reached the top of the trail?"

The sky had been there. Leaves hushing and shushing. "I don't know."

"What do you mean, you don't know?" Adam asked. "Mags, it just happened, like—"

"I don't know!" I yanked away from Adam, pressing myself into the tree, trying to find my way through it and to the other side. "I-don't-know-I-don't-know-I-don't-know-I-don't—"

"Okay, okay," Adam pulled me to him. His chest was sticky and warm, and he smelled like summer. "It's okay. You don't have to tell me anything."

"I can't," I said. "I can't remember. Just the kiss. And the screaming."

Adam grabbed my hands as I jerked away. He looked me in the eyes again. "Mags. You have to pull it together, okay?"

I nodded.

"We have to go back down."

"I'm not jumping," I said, tasting the terror in my words. "I can't jump."

"We'll take the trail down. Pete went to get help, so when we—"

"Help?"

"For Joey."

"Why does Joey need help?" I asked, feeling something inside me coil up tight.

"Oh, Mags." Adam pulled me to him again, squishing my nose against his shoulder. It hurt. Everything hurt.

"I want to leave," I said. "I want to go home."

He rocked me, back and forth.

I wrapped my arms around his shoulders. "What's going on, Adam?"

"Let's go down. We'll figure everything out."

"Did I—I mean, I didn't—"

"How about this," Adam pulled me up, shoving the leafy arms of the brush away, and tugged me to the trail, "you just keep quiet. Let me do all the talking."

I nodded. Wiped my nose and realized my whole face was wet. Was I crying?

And then we were moving through the woods, back to the top of the cliff. Toward the screaming, which was softer now, but not gone like I needed it to be.

"I can't," I said, pulling away, wanting to run again. "I can't go down there."

Adam grabbed my arm, his fingers wrapping around my skin like a vine from one of the trees surrounding us, and wouldn't let me go. "We have to."

"I'm taking her to the car," Adam said as we stepped from the bridge of rocks to the other side of the bank.

Shannon's eyes were wide, glossy, and Tanna's arm, which was wrapped around her waist, looked to be the only thing holding her up.

"Are you okay, Maggie?" Tanna's braids dripped. Trembled with her body.

Shannon scraped her hands through her hair. She looked around, her eyes searching for something that wasn't there.

"I don't under—"

"She's not hurt." Adam squeezed my arm. He hadn't let go. Not once the whole way down. "But I'm getting her out of here. Pete can lead the paramedics back. Okay?"

"Go through the grove," Tanna said, her eyes darting toward the circle of trees behind her. "Not past the . . ."

Adam nodded.

I looked at them all, the way their eyes had turned dark, their faces shadowed with something that had nothing to do with sunlight.

With one swift breath, I pulled away, yanking my arm from Adam's grip so quickly that he didn't have time to respond. And then I was running again. But this time, not away.

At first I looked at the water, expecting to see Joey floating on his back, spitting a glittering fountain up into the air the way he had earlier. I thought of him popping up, winking, and yelling, *Gotcha!* Because that's the kind of guy he was. Always joking. Playing. Trying to make someone laugh.

17

But he wasn't there. Not in the water.

The towels were still laid out. The one Joey and I had shared. Tanna's. Adam's.

I found Joey, too.

That stopped me.

He was lying there.

Motionless.

One arm flung wide.

I was confused, trying to figure out what had happened to Shannon's yellow towel. Because it was gone. Replaced by another that I had never seen.

Or was it?

No. Just different, soaked in something dark and sticky.

"Joey?"

As the word escaped my mouth, I felt Adam yanking me back, twisting me around and pulling me tight against him so that the only thing I could see was the sway of the treetops.

"We have to go, Maggie. You can't be here."

"But, Joey—"

"He's gone, Mags." Adam's voice was hoarse. Broken. "I'm so sorry, but he's gone."

"You're lying!" I tried to push Adam away, to break free of him, but he was too strong. And my body wasn't working right. I was shaky, and unstable, and dizzy all at the same time. "He's right there!"

Adam spun me around and I jumped up on him, digging my elbows into his shoulders and neck. It was the only thing I could think to do. And it worked. From over his head, I caught one last glimpse of Joey.

That's all it took.

I might not have understood everything at that point. But Joey's head didn't look right. It was misshapen. Concave at the temple.

And I knew Adam was telling the truth.

A shriek hit the rock wall, bouncing around several times before I realized it had come from my mouth. Adam yanked me down, jerking me toward the trail. Swiping our backpacks from their perch against a tree, he flung them both over his shoulder.

"They're coming. We have to go."

"Who's coming?" I asked, trying frantically to string everything together so it would make sense while, at the same time, trying to push it all away. It felt like I was swimming through the scene, like I was in an underwater movie that I couldn't control. But then I heard them.

Sirens.

They were getting closer.

"You're not ready to talk to anyone, Mags," Adam said firmly.

My hip bumped hard against a large tree as I tried to twist out of his grasp again, the rough bark scraping at my skin.

"You have to come with me." Adam turned back, flashing me a frenzied look. "Please."

There was something in his face, his eyes, that kept me from resisting. It was like Adam was the only real thing left in my world. And I trusted him. I had since second grade when he helped me up after I'd fallen from a swing on the playground. Everyone was laughing at me because they'd seen my Hello Kitty underwear, but Adam, who was way cool even for a second grader, had told them to stop, and they'd listened. He had, after all, just beat out every fifth grader in the schoolwide Hula Hoop contest.

If he wanted to take control now and tell me what to do, I needed to listen.

We moved through the trees, silent but for our rushed breathing and the soft crunch of our footsteps on the trail.

The sirens got louder. Closer.

We reached the end of the trail at the same time that the ambulance pulled into the parking lot. Adam stopped, backing into me, the zipper from my purple backpack biting into the skin of my arm.

"What're you doing?" I asked. "We have to—"

"Shh!" In one swift movement, Adam turned, wrapped his hand over my mouth, and pulled me into the line of trees, ducking us behind the largest, which stood only a few feet from the trail.

Pete yelled over the cries of the siren. I heard words like *cliff*, *jump*, and *ledge*. There were steady shouts back and forth as the paramedics realized they'd have to hike into the woods to reach the injured person they were there to help.

And then I heard the worst thing of all. The word I'd been trying to claw from my mind since the moment I'd seen Joey lying still on that towel.

"We tried CPR," Pete called out as he started down the trail, racing just ahead of two uniformed men who were carrying a backboard and large bags filled with medical supplies. "I think he's dead."

3

The Whole Spinning World

The quilt my grandmother made for my parents when they were first married covered my legs. I sat on the plush couch in my living room, imagining all the things that could be damaging the fabric her fingers had lovingly sewn together: greasy sunscreen, algae from the water at the gorge, cigarette ash, beer I'd spilled on myself when Tanna cracked a joke and made me laugh too hard. But those were the easy things.

There was also sweat, vomit, and blood. Rubbing off my skin. Soaking into the blanket to forever become part of its makeup. Tainting the patch of yellow flowered fabric from the dress my mother wore on her first day of school, sullying the blue-striped swatch that came from my grandfather's favorite flannel shirt, contaminating the oldest square, a piece of scratchy gray wool from my great-grandmother's fanciest Sunday dress.

"What are you saying?" My mother's voice came from the entry, her words high-pitched and staccato quick, stabbing every inch of me.

Adam answered, but his voice was so hushed I couldn't make out his reply.

A choked sound escaped my mother.

And I knew that she knew.

I squeezed my eyes shut, gripping the fabric of the blanket in my hands as if it had the magical power to transport me back in time. Not far. Just to late last night. After Dutton's party. When Joey stood on my doorstep, glowing in the faint light of the moon, his brown hair mussed, his thick hands engulfing mine.

"Tomorrow's gonna be awesome," he'd said with a grin. "And Monday night at Shan's, even better."

If only I had known then as I'd stood there with him. Joey was all out of Monday nights.

I sucked in a shaky breath and tried to remember every detail of our last moments alone—the crickets crying out to the cool spring air, a gentle breeze that carried the tangy scent of the earth, the feel of Joey's cotton shirt, soft against my cheek as we wrapped our arms around each other.

He'd stopped me as I pulled away, looking right into my eyes, placing a finger under my chin and tipping my head back slightly. He smiled in that crooked way of his.

"You happy?" he'd asked. "With me, I mean?"

An easy laugh worked its way from my lips. "Couldn't be happier," I'd said. And then I had leaned in, closing my eyes, tasting him before our lips even met. It was lazy and sweet, our last real kiss. So unlike our very first. I felt safe and sure, because I knew everything that mattered, I felt it deep inside. Joey was mine.

Joey tugged his favorite Adidas baseball cap from his

22

back pocket, pulling it on as he walked back to his black truck, which he'd parked cockeyed in the street. He stopped and looked at me one last time, tossing his hand in the air before hopping into the driver's seat. I stood watching as he drove away.

Shannon, who sat in the passenger seat, tipped her head against the glass of the window, her silver barrette straining for release. Joey turned the radio on, and Pete, in the truck's bed, nodded his head to the beat of a sleepy song that I couldn't quite make out. The music streamed through the back windows like strands of thick velvet ribbon, trailing into the deep blue-black of the night. I watched until the taillights turned the corner at the end of my street, wishing for nothing in particular. Because I didn't know that I needed to.

If only there had been some kind of sign. If only *something* had made me insist we change our plans. If only I'd kept Joey away from the gorge. He would be safe.

With me.

But now he was gone.

My whole body ached with the thought that I would never see him again.

Never. Again.

"So you just *left*?" my father asked.

Adam's muffled answer rushed from his lips.

Something inside me broke open. I bent forward, bringing the blanket to my face, burying myself into its history, smothering the awful sounds that poured from my body.

It's not real. It's not real. It's not real. It can't be real.

23

I squeezed harder. My eyes. My fingers on the blanket.

I shoved my mind out of the room, away from the moment.

Taking a deep breath, I thought of towering trees, the way they swayed in the breeze. But that took me right back to the gorge. Next I saw a flash of pinwheels, multicolored, spinning and spinning and spinning in the front garden of the house on the corner, the last turn before the gorge entrance. But that made me wonder if Joey had seen them, if those twirling colors had been one of the last things his eyes took in. So I envisioned a night sky, so big it could swallow any problem, whisk it away. But then I remembered the evening Joey and I lay on our backs in the bed of his truck, staring up as shooting stars streaked across the dusky canvas above us.

That was the first night.

I couldn't believe we'd just had our last.

But more than anything, I couldn't believe I'd just left him at the gorge. He'd been hurt. And I'd abandoned him.

I had to go back.

I swung my legs over the side of the couch, yanking at the quilt, tearing it off my body. But my bare feet were caught in the fabric, tripped up by all the history it contained, and I slid to the ground in a shivering heap.

"Joey," I said, my voice a hoarse whisper. "Joey?"

My hands were frantic, shaky, and numb as I clawed at the fabric that trapped me. I kicked my legs out, flinging the little squares of the past into the air. I heard a loud ripping sound and didn't understand enough to care. I needed to be free. To go back. To be with him.

I pulled myself upright just as my mother, my father, and Adam rushed from the entry into the living room.

"Maggie." My mother's voice shook.

"You're okay," my father said, walking to me and kissing the top of my head. He lingered, his hand gripping my shoulder like he was afraid to let go.

"No," I said. "I'm not." I pulled away from him, stumbling into the coffee table. Adam grabbed my elbow, steadying me so I didn't tumble back to the floor.

My father's eyes blinked furiously as he ran his hand along his stubbled chin. "Honey, I think you need to sit down."

"Maggie." My mother dropped to the couch, patting the cushion beside her, her brown eyes glistening with so much emotion, I had to look away. The quilt lay in a messy heap at her feet. "Please have a seat. We need to talk."

"I'm not talking." I shook my head, my hair whipping around my shoulders. "I have to go back." I looked at Adam, whose hands were clasped together in one giant fist. His eyes glimmered with tears, the kind that didn't spill over. The kind that let you know something still didn't feel quite real. "You have to take me back."

"Mags, we can't just—"

"What if we were wrong? What if he's still alive? I don't want him to wake up and wonder where I am. What if he's—" I choked then, on my words, on the heaviness twisting through me. I looked at Adam and saw the way he'd squeezed his eyes shut, trying to block me from his mind. "What if he's *scared*?" I asked, my voice streaking through the room, trying to find a place to hide.

"Sweetie." My mother stood, placing her hands on my shoulders. "You need to sit down."

I yanked away from her. My feet tangled in the blanket again, and I crashed to the floor. Adam's hands were on me before I even registered what had happened, and he pulled me up. He'd always been steady and strong. So very alive.

I didn't want to be there. Not anymore. Not with any of them.

I pushed my way past Adam, through the foyer, and bounced off the doorjamb as I made my way out the front door, stumbling down the porch steps to the walkway.

This time I didn't make it far. Adam, again. He caught me.

I was spinning. The whole world was spinning. And I wondered if that's how it had felt for Joey.

My breath exploded out of me as I hit the ground, Adam on top of me. Sticky prickles of grass and blinding sunlight invaded my senses, bringing me back to reality, sucking me under waves of pain.

Adam pressed his heaving chest into mine. Tears streamed from his eyes onto my cheeks, chin, and neck.

"Maggie," he whispered, "he's gone."

I shook my head, straining against the tears that burned my own eyes.

Adam buried his face in my neck, his hot, heavy sobs drowning me.

I looked straight at the sun, the burning, spiraling sun, and hated every wave of its energy. If only it had hidden behind a thick batch of storm clouds today, we never would have gone to the gorge. If not for that faraway star, Joey would still be alive.

My father peeled Adam and me from the sticky ground, balancing us as we shuffled to the house. My mother was waiting with the quilt, and she draped it over me when I sat on the couch next to Adam. I watched my father go for the phone, pick it up, and dial. Then he disappeared into his office, his voice trailing behind him as someone answered on the other end of the line. I looked down and saw my knee poking through a gaping hole that sliced through the patches of fabric.

"Mom," I said, sucking in a deep breath. "I ruined Grandma's quilt."

My mother patted the bare skin of my knee. "That can be fixed."

Adam's parents arrived less than fifteen minutes after my father called them. Twelve, to be exact. I knew because I'd been staring at the clock like it was the only tether still tying me to Joey, even if each second ticked me farther and farther away from the last moment I had had with him. My last moment with Joey. Nothing about that thought felt real.

"Adam! Oh, dear God, thank you." Mrs. Meacham rushed to the couch and wrapped her arms around Adam, pulling him close. Mr. Meacham kneeled in front of them and hugged them together. "You're okay?" Adam's mother leaned back and looked Adam up and down.

"There's blood," Mr. Meacham said, gently gripping Adam's arm and inspecting his skin.

"It's not mine." Adam rubbed at the spot and then quickly pulled his hand away.

"Oh, God." Mrs. Meacham melted into the couch cushion, holding her hand to her heart, her brown curls quivering. "Joey. I feel like that boy is one of my own, you two have been friends for so long. I have no idea how Trisha and Mike are going to handle the news."

I closed my eyes at the thought of Joey's parents. I saw them in a hundred different ways all at once: playing cards at the dining room table, sitting together on the porch swing, reading on the back patio. Smiling. They were always smiling. Pressing my fingertips into my eyes, I erased their happy faces, groaning at the thought of them hearing the news. Would the police just knock on their door and tell them that their son had died?

"Mom." Adam gripped my hand in his, pulling my fingers away from my eyes. "Can you *not* do that right now?"

"Oh." Mrs. Meacham wiped tears from her face and sucked in a deep breath. "I'm sorry. I just . . . Do they know yet? Has anyone called them?"

"We figured it would be best if we let the police handle that," my father said. "Since we don't know exactly what's going on."

"You told us they left the scene," Mr. Meacham said. "Is that true?" Mr. Meacham looked from Adam to me and back again.

"Yeah," Adam nodded, looking to the ground. "I had to . . . Maggie couldn't stay, Dad. I had to get her out of there."

"I just don't understand how you could leave Joey—"

"I didn't *leave* Joey, Dad." Adam's voice shook with

anger. "There was nothing I could do for him. But Maggie needed my help."

"Maggie was the only person on top of the cliff with Joey when it happened," my father said. "She doesn't remember anything. At least nothing significant. I think Adam was focused on getting her away as fast as he could, to keep her from seeing . . . anything."

"It's like I was losing her, too," Adam whispered, squeezing my hand. I squeezed back and tugged away quickly, unsure why the action sent an electric jolt up my arm. "It scared me when she couldn't remember, how she couldn't answer any of my questions. I was afraid of what might happen if she stayed with him. Joey was so . . . still. And I knew he wouldn't want her there."

Adam's words tripped me up. I remembered when he first found me in the woods. The vision was a quick flash, but his eyes came back to me, how the swirling currents of green were wild with something that ran much deeper than fear. Everything else had faded into a dark, shadowy nothing.

"Thank you," I said, my voice soft. "For taking care of me."

A silence that felt like a heavy weight blanketed the room, and I wished I'd just kept my mouth shut. I wondered if we were all thinking the same thing: *Why didn't anyone take care of Joey?*

"You can't recall anything, dear?" Mrs. Meacham's voice was tinged with pleading. It made me want to scream.

I shook my head.

"She can remember some of the stuff that happened

right before they climbed up the trail," Adam said. "But nothing else."

"I'm sure it's the shock." Mrs. Meacham looked at my mom and shook her head. "Nothing to worry about."

"What about you?" Mr. Meacham tilted his head toward Adam. "What do you remember?"

Adam's eyes flitted to me, and then quickly away. "Dad, now's not the time to—"

"It's fine." I wasn't sure if that was true or not, but I needed to find out. "I want to know, too."

Adam sighed and leaned forward, propping his elbows on his knees. He didn't look at anyone, just the ground, as he started talking.

"We all saw Joey and Maggie when they got to the top of the cliff. They walked out to the edge, like always, to make sure the water was clear. Maggie looked a little pale, kind of freaked, and Joey was talking to her."

I strained, trying to remember. What had Joey said? What had happened in those last minutes? No matter how hard I tried, I couldn't see Joey. Couldn't remember one single word he had said.

"They turned, and we waited. Just like always. Then, a minute or two later, Joey flew over the edge. But that part wasn't like always. He was kind of twisted, his fall was awkward."

"What exactly do you mean by awkward?" Mr. Meacham asked.

"Off balance. His arms were spread out. Like he was trying to steady himself. But he couldn't do it in time. And he hit the ledge."

I pulled my legs to my chest and wrapped my arms around them, burying my face in the patches of old fabric that I'd pulled over my knees. Joey hit the ledge?

"His head." Adam's words were hoarse. Strained. "He hit the ledge with the side of his head. And then he was in the water. We all raced out to get him—everyone except Shannon, who grabbed a phone—and got him to the bank as fast as we could."

What had I been doing? I asked myself. *While my friends were trying to save my boyfriend's life, where was I? Why hadn't I scrambled down to help?*

"When we realized there was nothing we could do, I climbed up to find Maggie. We'd been calling to her, but she hadn't answered. I found her a good way from the cliff, hiding just off the trail. And when she said she didn't remember anything, I panicked."

As I listened to Adam's shaking voice, I wasn't so sure if I ever wanted to remember. Remembering might make everything feel worse than it already did. And I wasn't sure I could handle that.

"Were you drinking?" Adam's father asked, his eyes tight.

"I don't think now is the time to delve into all of that," my father said.

"There is no better time." Mr. Meacham shoved a hand in the pocket of his tan golf shorts. "The police will be asking the kids all kinds of questions in the very near future."

My stomach dropped and the room started to spin. "I don't want to talk to the police," I said, tilting my head up from my knees even though I felt as if I might be sick.

"I don't mean to sound harsh, Maggie, but you're not going to have a choice." Mr. Meacham pinched the bridge of his nose. "And the first thing they're going to ask is why you two left the scene."

Adam looked at me. "I'm sorry," he said. "I thought I was doing the right thing."

"We appreciate you taking care of our daughter," my mother said to Adam, her voice soft, reassuring. "Don't you two worry about anything. The police will ask a few questions and leave. They have to follow procedure. Nothing will come of it."

I took a deep breath, hoping she was right. Hoping they would accept the fact that I didn't remember anything. Because after hearing Adam's version of what happened, I decided that I didn't want to recall my own memories. No matter who wanted to know, I wasn't about to try to sort through the jumble of flashes and put it all back together again. If it were up to me, I would erase every moment that happened after Joey kissed me on those rocks. If I could, I might even erase myself.

"If it's all right with you, I'm going to take Maggie upstairs," my mother said. "A nice warm shower and—"

"No!" I sat forward, looking right at Adam. "I want to stay with Adam."

"I think it's best if we take Adam home," Mr. Meacham said.

"I'm not going anywhere," Adam insisted.

My father cleared his throat. "What if we call the police? Making the first contact might be the smartest choice, letting them know we're willing to help in any way we can. We could tell them they can stop by and speak to the kids together."

I nodded. Anything to keep Adam from leaving. I felt like he was the only thing holding me together, and I was scared that if he was gone everything left of me would crumble into a fine dust.

"It might be a good idea." Mrs. Meacham looked at her husband. "We don't want them to think we're hiding anything."

"They're not going to come here," Mr. Meacham said. "They'll want to question the kids at the station."

"You watch entirely too much television, dear," Mrs. Meacham said. "I'm sure, under the circumstances, they'll be happy to come to the house."

"I'll call them now," my father said.

I looked up at Adam's face, at his shimmering eyes, and had an overwhelming need to touch him. To make sure he was real. Because nothing in my world felt real anymore. It all seemed like a dirty trick someone was playing to get back at me for something. Trouble was, I couldn't figure out what.

I reached out and grabbed onto Adam's wrist and felt the pulse of blood flowing through his body. He looked at my hand and then covered it with his own.

Holding on to him, staring at the frayed edges of the ripped quilt, I focused all of my fading energy on keeping that moment from turning into the next.

4

Hands Clasped Tight

"What are we gonna say?" I whispered as two uniformed police officers walked past the chairs where Adam and I were seated. It was a wide hall in the entry of the police station, the tiled floor a marbled gray and white that looked like it would be cold against the bottoms of my feet if I kicked off my flip-flops.

"What do you mean?" Adam looked at me, his eyes scrunched tight. The officers' footsteps slammed against the walls, echoing like the gorge, vibrating my entire body. "We're gonna tell the truth."

I pressed myself against the straight back of the chair, trying to mold my body to the hard surface. "Right."

"We don't have anything to hide." Adam's foot, which had been tap-tap-tapping the floor nervously, suddenly stopped. He swiveled in his seat and leaned toward me, his eyes searching mine. "Do we?"

Adam's hand gripped my knee, and I placed my hand

over his, soaking in the warmth of his skin, reassured that he was sitting there next to me. Alive.

"Mags." Adam ran a hand through the dried clumps of his sun-streaked hair. "If I should know something, *now* is the time to tell me. They're gonna be done talking to our parents any minute, and—"

"There's nothing more to say." My bangs fell forward and I swiped them out of my eyes, blinking away the fear that had taken hold of me, and settled even deeper into the raw pain of Joey's sudden absence. "I can't remember anything."

"You really can't?" Adam pressed his lips together so tightly they disappeared. He quivered a little, and for a moment, he looked like the kindergarten version of himself, lost and alone, like he had when his mother dropped him off for his first day of school. I squeezed his hand, the way I had all those years ago when I'd led him to the reading corner to distract him from being left behind.

I closed my eyes, playing the day's events along the backs of my lids like a silent movie. Driving in Tanna's car, windows down, music blaring, watching Shannon's hair whip, and dip, and flip all around her head in the crazy, rushing wind as she giggled about how Ronnie Booker had puked all over Gina Hanlon's purse at the party we'd gone to the night before. Hiking up the trail from the parking lot to the Jumping Hole, the rush of a cool breeze against my skin. Feet running, pounding, crashing.

My eyes snapped open and I sucked in a deep breath. It felt like I was underwater, struggling to find my way to the surface.

"What?" Adam asked, his eyes wide. "Did you remember something?"

"Feet," I said. "Running and—"

The door to the room where the detectives had taken our parents swung open with a loud *click-swoosh*, and the gruff voice of the detective, who reminded me of a gorilla, chased my found memory back into hiding.

All that was left was the fear. And the comfort of not knowing.

They filed out of the room in pairs, the two detectives, my mom and dad, Mr. and Mrs. Meacham. Our parents looked like deflated shells of their usual selves. I saw it in their eyes, the way their heads hung low, how their shoulders slumped with exhaustion, like two hours of this news was already too much for them to bear. If there was hope there, masked by the emotion that threatened to suck them under, I couldn't find it.

When they saw us, their feet stuttered. Stopped.

The long, flowy skirt my mother wore swayed around her legs as if a strong wind had just drifted through. I heard a slight grunt escape Adam's father's lips.

The detectives just stared, taking us in.

Me.

Adam.

Our heads bowed together.

Hands clasped tight.

And the way we practically clung to each other like our individual survival depended on the connection.

It was as if they'd been able to forget reality for a moment, to place it in the dark corner of a high shelf while they dealt with the formalities. But seeing Adam and me shifted things, brought it all spilling down, nearly knocking them to the ground.

"We're very sorry for your loss, Maggie." Detective Wallace looked at me, creases wrinkling the loose skin on his face. "Your parents told us that you and Joey had been dating for the last two years."

"*Almost* two years." I pressed my fingers into my eyes, realizing they were leaking again. "Would have been two years this fall."

My mother handed me a tissue, then placed a hand on my knee.

"We asked you here so you can help us piece together the events of the day. We need you to tell us everything you can about what led to Joey's accident." Detective Meyer shifted in his seat. His large body strained the chair beneath him, causing it to moan in protest.

I took in a shaky breath. "I can't remember much," I said, wishing they'd allowed Adam and me to be questioned together, wondering what they'd asked him while he was sitting at this very table with his own parents just ten minutes ago. We'd passed one another as he exited the interrogation room and I entered, his eyes saying a thousand things at once: be calm; that was brutal; you can do this; I hate these men. He'd grabbed my hand and given it a quick squeeze before the detectives rushed him along with a firm reminder that we were to be questioned

37

separately. And now, without Adam by my side, I felt lost.

My father cleared his throat, and I realized I hadn't really answered. "After the climb up the trail, everything just kind of disappears."

Detective Wallace's mouth twitched, the thick gray moustache on his upper lip looking like a caterpillar wiggling to free itself from a prison. "Your parents explained that already, Maggie. Occasionally, in the event of a trauma, a person will suffer from memory loss. You'll probably begin to recall the day in bits and pieces. You can give us more information as it returns to you. For now, we would like for you to tell us what you *do* remember."

I looked from one detective to the other, hating the way their eyes pierced my skin. "Okay."

"Let's start with the easy stuff." Detective Meyer flipped through a small spiral notebook and tugged a pen from the inside pocket of his suit jacket. "When did you arrive at the gorge?"

I looked at my father whose face somehow seemed ten years older than it had when he'd sat across the table from me earlier in the morning as we ate a blueberry pancake and bacon breakfast.

"It was a little after eleven," I said. "We wanted to be all set up by noon, to get the best sun."

"And when you say 'we,' who are you referring to?" Detective Wallace asked.

"Me, Tanna, Shannon, Pete, Adam, and . . . Joey." My voice broke when I said his name.

"What would you say Joey's demeanor was when you arrived?"

"He was just Joey." I closed my eyes and remembered the way the sunlight framed him after his first jump. He'd stood above me, shaking water from his hair all over me as I lay on the towel. I'd giggled. Kicked him away. I wanted to scream at myself for that. I should have pulled him closer and never let go.

I took in a deep slicing breath as I remembered his smile. The sound of his laughter. "He was joking. Laughing. Like always."

"So you wouldn't say he seemed depressed. Or angry about anything? Maybe a fight with his parents? His brother? Or . . . anyone else?"

"No." I blinked several times, something else in my memory shifting just out of reach. "Summer's about to start. . . . We're almost seniors. He was as far from depressed as a person can get."

"Can you walk us through the events leading to Joey's accident?" Detective Wallace asked. "Tell us everything you remember?"

"We were just hanging out," I said. "Listening to music. Tanna, Shannon, and I were lying out on our towels, getting into the water when we were too hot. The guys went up and made several jumps. Tanna and Shannon jumped, too. Once each, I think."

"But not you?" Detective Meyer asked, his eyebrows pulling inward.

I shook my head. "I've never jumped off the cliff."

Detective Meyer jotted something down on the paper in front of him, then looked me directly in the eyes. "Why not?"

I shrugged. "Too afraid."

"I see," Detective Wallace said. "So what made you go up with Joey? We were told that you intended to jump together. Is this true?"

Shannon's face flashed in front of me. *I dare you,* she'd taunted, a giggle escaping her lips as she grabbed the bottle of tequila planted at the head of the towels and took a long swig.

"It was a dare," I said. "I've tried to jump before. It's like a running joke. That I'm too afraid."

"Who dared you?" Detective Wallace asked.

"Shannon."

Detective Meyer wrote the name in his notebook.

"And what made you decide to try again? What made you feel like you could do it today?"

"I don't know," I said, remembering Joey's smile, the feel of his skin sliding against mine as he tucked my arm against his body and we began walking toward the bridge of rocks.

"Was it the alcohol?" Detective Meyer asked. "We found a bottle of tequila at the scene."

The scene? I cringed at the word. Blue Springs Gorge, our most sacred hangout, had become a crime scene.

"How much did Joey have to drink?" Detective Wallace asked.

My eyes stuttered between the two men's faces, their features blurring into a shadowy puzzle.

"We'll find out for ourselves when the results from the autopsy come back," Detective Meyer said.

"Autopsy?" The word whirred through my brain, flipping

around and around. That meant they were going to cut Joey open.

"Yes." Detective Wallace's lip twitched again and I had an urge to pluck the hairs from his face. "In the case of an accidental death we always order an autopsy. And we run through a complete investigation."

"He'd had a little to drink," I said, recalling the way Joey had stumbled as he walked out of the water the last time.

"Would you say he was intoxicated?" Detective Wallace asked.

I shook my head. "I don't know."

"You're aware that we just finished interviewing your friend Adam. He told us that Joey was a daredevil," Detective Wallace said with a sad smile. "That he often showed off, performing stunts when he jumped from the cliff."

I pictured Joey at the top of the cliff, smiling down at us, his arms spread wide. *Watch this,* he'd yelled just before disappearing. Seconds later, he reappeared, soaring out from the lip of the cliff, his body circling over itself in a flip before he slipped into the water with barely a splash. Had that been his second or third jump of the day?

"Yeah," I said. "Joey liked attention."

"Can you describe your relationship with Joey?" Detective Meyer asked. "Would you say that the two of you were happy?"

I closed my eyes briefly, remembering my plan to spend the night with him in just a few weeks. "We were very happy," I said.

"What about your relationship with the rest of your friends?" Detective Meyer asked. "It seems as if you are all very close."

My father cleared his throat. "These kids have all grown up together, Detective. They've known one another since kindergarten."

"That's a lot of history." Detective Wallace scrunched his lips in a sympathetic pout.

Detective Meyer scribbled more words on the paper in front of him. I wanted to rip the notepad out of his hand, to tear the flimsy paper from the wire spiral. How could my life—and Joey's death—be whittled down to just a few words?

"We're trying to figure something out," Detective Wallace said. "And we'd like your help, Maggie."

"Okay," I said, drawing the word out so it sounded more like a question.

"We don't understand why you and Adam left the scene." Detective Meyer's voice suddenly sounded very official. Almost demanding.

My heart started beating more rapidly. I felt hot. Stifling hot. I shifted in my seat, and my mother's hand squeezed my knee again.

"Maggie?" Detective Meyer said. "Can you explain that for us?"

I shook my head. "I don't know."

"You don't know why you left?" Detective Meyer's voice was tight with something I couldn't place. Irritation. Maybe anger. "Or you don't know if you can explain it?"

"Adam was looking out for our daughter," my mother

said. "He was the one to find her after Joey's fall. Maggie was in shock, and it scared him when she claimed to have no memory of what had happened. He thought it was best to bring her straight home."

The detectives looked at each other. Then they stared at me.

"Can you tell us the first thing you remember?" Detective Wallace asked. "*After* Joey's fall?"

I looked at the table in front of me, my eyes following the swirls in the wood, shuffling through the memories I had, trying to categorize them into *before* and *after*.

"The seat belt clicking into place," I said. "Adam's hand."

"Adam put your seat belt on?" Detective Meyer asked. "Good. That's very good. What else?"

"The quilt my grandmother made. Spread across my lap. And whispering."

"That was right after she came home," my mother said. "She sat on the couch while Adam told us what happened."

"You must be grateful that Adam is such a caring young man," Detective Meyer said, looking at my parents.

"Yes." My mother straightened herself in her chair and smoothed one hand down the side of her brown hair. "We feel very fortunate that our daughter had someone looking out for her best interests today."

Detective Meyer leaned forward, his hulking chest creating a shadow on the table in front of him, blanketing the words he'd written on the paper.

I looked at my dad. He steepled his fingers under his

chin. "Can you explain what happens from here? You said something about an autopsy?"

The detectives exchanged a glance, and then turned to my father. "Yes. Though this appears, in all respects, to be an accidental death, it's standard to open an official investigation. It is our job to learn everything we can about exactly what happened today so we can consider *everything* that might have led to the accident." Detective Wallace spread his hands in the air.

Detective Meyer agreed with a curt nod. "We will be searching Joey's car and bedroom, looking over his phone records, and cross-referencing the statements from all of our interviews, which will also include friends who were not at the scene, to get the most detailed picture of his last twenty-four hours. Only then can we close the investigation."

"So—" I said, trying to think of anything but the words that were ringing through my head: *death, accident, autopsy*. "This is, like, a full-on investigation?"

"Yes," Detective Wallace said. "It is."

My mother's fingers dug into my knee.

"And we have one more very important question for you at this time." Detective Meyer looked directly into my eyes. "Where was Joey last night?"

"A party," I said with a sigh. "We were all at the party."

"Yes." Detective Wallace nodded. "Jimmy Dutton's. We're aware of the party."

"We'd like to know where Joey was *after* the party," Detective Meyer said.

"He took me home," I said. "And then dropped off

Shannon and Pete. He was probably home by twelve thirty."

The two detectives stared at me. Hard. And then they looked at each other. I was almost certain that Detective Wallace shrugged his shoulders, but the movement was so slight I couldn't be sure.

Something inside me started to backpedal, like I was mentally trying to escape. But I didn't move fast enough.

"No"—Detective Meyer cleared his throat and turned his eyes to me again—"Joey did not make it home last night."

My thoughts stretched back to the previous evening, which now felt like it had happened in some alternate lifetime. I went back to the kiss on my front porch. Watching Joey drive away. Hearing the music stream from the windows of his truck. What would have kept him from going home?

"I'm not sure that I understand why this is important." My mother sat forward in her seat, tipping her head sideways. "What does last night have to do with today's accident?"

"As I already explained, Mrs. Reynolds, we're trying to construct a detailed time line of Joey's last twenty-four hours of life." Detective Meyer watched me closely as he spoke. "It's standard procedure, I assure you. We simply need to know where Joey was during the overnight hours."

"There's a mistake, or something." I shook my head. "I already told you. Joey dropped me off a little after midnight. He took Shannon and Pete home. And then he went home."

Detective Wallace shook his head slowly. "No, Maggie. He did not go home."

"He said . . ." Everything in my head jumbled together. I wasn't sure if I knew anything anymore. If Joey was out all night, why hadn't he said anything? We'd hung out at the gorge for hours; Joey had plenty of opportunities to share if he'd been out all night doing something crazy. It's the kind of thing he'd usually brag about. . . . But he hadn't mentioned a thing. "He had to have been at home."

Detective Meyer leaned toward me, lowering his voice. "We've spoken with his parents. They are certain that he spent the night out, and that he wasn't where he said he would be."

"Maggie, do you have any idea where he might have gone?" Detective Wallace asked. "Or who he might have been with?"

I opened my mouth, searching for anything that might answer the very same questions that had started to spin around in my own mind. But I had no answers, so all that came out was a choppy, stuttering sound that hardly reminded me of my own voice.

"This is an awful lot to take in," my mother said, squeezing my knee again. "If Maggie remembers anything, we'll be sure to call you." From my mother's tone, it was obvious that the conversation was over. But I suddenly didn't want it to be.

"You're *sure* he didn't go home?" I asked, focusing on the sound of the words tumbling out of me instead of the fact that, if they were true, it meant Joey had been keeping some kind of secret.

Both detectives nodded, eyes trained on me. "Positive," Detective Wallace answered.

I looked down at my hands, squeezing them together so tightly they turned a sickly whitish-blue. I wasn't sure if I was angry with Joey for keeping a secret or glad to realize that maybe he could go on living through all the little things I didn't yet know. Things that I could easily find out.

"I assume it is standard, in cases like this, for people to obtain lawyers," my father said, placing a hand on my shoulder. "If you believe you may need to question Margaret again, we will certainly call our attorney."

"That would be fine with us." Detective Wallace met my father's eyes.

"Just so you know," Detective Meyer said, "we will be requesting that Maggie undergo a medical and psychological exam in the next week or so."

"I'm not hurt." I pushed my chair back, standing, wavering a little, and placed my hand on the table for balance. "I don't need to see a doctor."

"But, Maggie, you *are* suffering from memory loss," Detective Wallace said. "This might actually help you."

"We will have our lawyer contact you for any further directions." My father stood, his chair scraping along the tiles of the floor.

My mother grabbed her purse from the floor and flung it onto her arm before she got to her feet.

Placing a hand on my back, my father led me toward the door. But I was still shaky and moved slowly as I tried to figure out what Joey could have been doing all night without me.

The detectives stood before I'd rounded the corner of the table. My fingers trailed the looping grain of the wood, and for some reason I didn't want to lose my connection with that cool surface.

But then I saw something that made me feel like racing from the room. As the detectives buttoned their suit jackets, like men always do when they stand, I sneaked a peek at their full uniforms, which hadn't really seemed like uniforms at all, since they were dressed like businessmen. But businessmen don't have handcuffs strapped to their waists, badges making their pockets bulge, or guns stuffed into holsters at their hips.

Suddenly, every fuzzy quality that had made the day feel like a dream slipped away from my consciousness. It was like I broke the surface of the water, my sight and hearing clearing in an instant. And for the first time since the accident, everything felt excruciatingly real.

Especially the thought of myself, alone in bed, while Joey was out in the dark night doing things without me. Things he obviously didn't want me to know about. And the gaping emptiness where my memories ought to be— memories of Joey's last moments on this earth, of our last moments together. There was so much that I suddenly needed to uncover, no matter the cost. Because learning all the things I didn't already know, finding a few more slices of life when Joey was with us, even if it only helped for a little while, was the only way I could cheat my way out of his death.

5

Waiting for His Touch

B there in 10 the text said. *T.*

I wasn't ready. Didn't know if I ever would be, but that wasn't what mattered.

I'd spent the last few hours sitting on the floor in my dark closet, knees pulled to my chest, remembering Saturday by sifting through the parts that hadn't disappeared. It had only been two days, but it felt more like forever.

After the police station, my parents called in a lawyer— a friend of a friend of my father's. With his stiffly combed hair and red-striped tie, I felt like Mr. Fontane had just stepped out of a movie of the week. I'd sat there in our living room as my parents spoke for me, silent except when I was asked a question, and then I only offered a *yes* or *no*.

My moment of clarity at the police station hadn't brought back any memories, hadn't answered any of the questions spinning around in my mind, spiraling out to the air around me. All I knew for sure was that the day's events were real. Something had happened. And Joey was gone.

To make matters worse, I had a feeling. A creeping feeling that slithered through the shadows of my heart, whispering to me when I was quiet—what if something I had done had killed Joey? What if something I didn't do could have saved him? And when I zoned out on the carpet or the drone of someone's voice, I saw flashes—treetops and tears and rippling water. I was afraid that if everything came flooding back, I'd face a truth that might be too much for me to handle. But even with all that fear, I wanted to pull the pieces together. The memories that had escaped me—I had to find them.

During a few quiet moments that first day, I'd wondered if it was real. The part where Joey had died. The part where I didn't. Maybe, in some parallel universe, Joey had survived and I was gone. Maybe my mom knew all about it, and that was why she had one hand on me every second she could. She thought I was fragile and wanted me by her side so she could keep me from imploding or exploding or whatever she was afraid might happen next.

My little secret: I was glad. It felt like she was keeping me from floating away. I was scared to death to leave the house without her. But this night, it was something I had to do. Something we all had to do. Together.

So I took a deep breath and slid out of the cocoon my closet had become, yanking my fingers through my tangled hair. As I pulled on a pair of jeans, I glanced in the mirror and saw the dark smearing shadows under my eyes. I ran a finger over the stitching on the front of Joey's baseball shirt: JOEY. It still smelled like him, and I pulled it on to feel like he was closer. Still with me.

I'd found the shirt in my car and remembered how he'd flung it into the backseat after school Friday (was that three days ago, or another lifetime?), claiming he was *hot-hot-hot*. With a smirk, I'd agreed. He'd flexed his arms dramatically before leaning toward me, nuzzling his face into my neck, knowing that tickle zone was the easiest way to make me laugh. My giggles mixed with his words, twining around them. *We're gonna have a kick-ass Memorial Day weekend,* he'd said. *Two parties and the gorge to kick off the best summer ever.* And then he'd kissed me, long and insistent, like he knew what I'd secretly planned for us when his parents left town in a few short weeks, and wanted to give me a prelude so I wouldn't back out.

When he pulled away, he cranked the dial on my radio until "Dynamite" by Taio Cruz pumped out the open windows and collided with everyone walking past. I reversed out of my parking space unaware that it would be the last time Joey would ever ride in my car.

When Joey's brother opened the front door of the Walthers' house I wanted to run. But I ignored that urge, because this night wasn't about me. My second impulse was to push past Rylan and rush up the staircase, to lock myself in Joey's room and bury myself in his blankets so I could feel him all around me one last time. But I didn't do that, either. Instead, I stepped into the foyer and wrapped my arms around Rylan's shoulders, pulling him close as everyone filed in behind me.

I breathed him in and held tight, not wanting to let go.

"This is one suck-ass Memorial Day, huh?" Pete asked, stepping around us and clapping Rylan on the shoulder.

As I pulled away, Rylan's lips turned up in an attempt at a smile. But it faded before it had the chance to form. Just two years younger, he reminded me so much of Joey—his sizzling blue eyes, his freckled nose, the curve of his chin—I had to look away, to search for something that might not hurt as much. But it didn't work. Joey was everywhere.

Resting on the entry table was a copy of *A Prayer for Owen Meany*, which Joey had been reading for English class. It sat as if he'd be back soon to pick it up and make his way through the last chapters. Perched on the staircase were his favorite Converse shoes, faded black with holes threatening the seams, one on its side, the laces flung loose. As if Joey would bound down the steps any minute to tug them on his feet before rushing out the door. They, too, seemed to be waiting for the touch of his hands.

"How are your parents?" Tanna asked, placing a hand on Rylan's back.

Rylan shook his head. "They're in the family room. I gotta warn you," he said, looking over his shoulder, toward the kitchen, "they're asking a lot of questions."

"Really?" Adam asked, looking up from the wood floor of the entry.

"Yeah, dude. They keep asking me where he was Friday night." Rylan's voice was a whisper. "Do any of you know—"

"Are they here, Rylan?" Joey's father asked, his voice

deep and raw, his words pulsing toward us from the family room. "We need some help with this."

"Look, if you know anything, just tell them," Rylan said. "And thanks for coming, guys. You have no idea how much it means to them. . . . To us."

"Bro," Pete said, wrapping an arm around Rylan's shoulders as we all moved toward the kitchen and living room, "where else would we be?"

"Yeah," Shannon said. "We're all family, Ry."

I imagined Joey by my side as we filed down the hallway and into the kitchen, rounding the bend into the cozy but enormous space of the Walthers' family room. It all looked so normal, it nearly killed me. Until I saw that nothing was normal at all. That was even worse.

Mr. and Mrs. Walther sat on the carpeted floor in front of a huge fireplace with pictures spread around the hearth in rippling waves. I wasn't so sure I could face those memories. But when Joey's parents stood and opened their arms to us, I didn't have a choice. I lost myself in their deep, shaking warmth, knowing that they felt the same pain that I did. A wall closed in behind me and I knew we'd all come together, huddled in the center of the room.

I'm not sure how long we stood like that, Shannon hugging my back, Pete tucked against my side, Tanna and Rylan pressed up against Mrs. Walther, Adam practically keeping Mr. Walther from collapsing to the floor. But I would have been okay if it had never ended. Really, it may have been better that way. But nothing stays the same in life.

"Imagine if he could see this." Adam broke the moment,

somehow finding the most fitting thing to say. "All of us standing here like a bunch of babies."

"He'd have our asses," Rylan said.

"Rylan!" Mrs. Walther's voice was so hoarse it made me cringe.

"Sorry, Ma. He'd have our *butts*. Is that better?"

"Don't be such a smart-ass," Mr. Walther said, ruffling Rylan's hair like he was still five.

We were pulling apart by then, wiping our faces with the palms of our hands, swiping at our noses, and moving toward the closest seats. As I sat between Pete and Shannon on the couch, I tried not to look down at the pictures. But that didn't work.

There was one of all of us from a football game sophomore year, faces painted with blue and black stripes, our arms up in the air as we screamed after a touchdown. A shot of Joey and me from prom. Another of him in his baseball uniform. Then there was one of Joey and Rylan from last year's family trip to Myrtle Beach, where just behind them, the sun plunged into the ocean.

"Those are just from the last few years," Mrs. Walther said, sitting cross-legged on the floor, wiping her raw nose with a tissue and clearing her throat. "Rylan's working on a slide show, but we'd also like to have several different posters for the funeral. I was thinking you guys could make a few."

"We can do whatever you need us to," Pete said, sliding off the couch and grabbing a picture. "These pictures are great. You guys remember this one?" He held the photo in the air, and there we were. All six of us, sitting on a floating dock in the middle of a wide, open lake. I stared at the way Joey had slung his arm lazily across my lap, wishing I could go back. The shot had been taken last summer, on the Fourth of July, when we'd gone to the lake with Pete's parents.

It all rushed back to me in a series of simple moments, the entire day speeding through my mind in an instant: lying out on the floating dock, the guys splashing us as they drove past on jet skis, Tanna's wild laughter, Shannon turning up the music when her favorite song came on the staticky radio. The smell of sunscreen and lake water, the salty taste of potato chips, and my fizzy, too-warm Coke. And later, the barbecue where Pete practically set all of our burgers on fire, and how Adam had saved the day by closing the lid, thick smoke drifting up toward the darkening sky. Tanna sitting on the steps to the deck, smiling about a new, secret boyfriend. And Joey, teasing her. His hands reaching for her phone, tugging at her hair, pulling her off the deck and throwing her over his shoulder, spinning her in circles, threatening that he wouldn't stop until he had a name. But he *had* stopped, his bare feet in the thick grass, as soon as she shouted that she was going to throw up all over him, and her secret had been saved. Shannon, watching everything as she walked under the trees, looking for the perfect marshmallow sticks to use for s'mores during the bonfire. And later still, the orange tint of the fire glowing as Joey pulled me away from the sounds of Pete's guitar and the singing voices of our friends as the first blasts of fireworks splashed through the sky.

"Remember the fireworks?" I asked. I could practically

feel their thunderous booms hitting me deep in the chest. One after another. And Joey's arms wrapped around my waist as we leaned against a tree near the shore.

"They were insane," Shannon said, but her voice was flat, like she didn't really believe herself.

It was quiet for a moment, Shannon's words echoing through the air. I wondered if we were all thinking the same thing. That we had been so lucky. And we hadn't even known it.

"My mom told me the funeral will be this Thursday," Adam said. He was rocking in a recliner next to the couch, clutching an oatmeal-colored pillow.

Mr. Walther took a deep breath. "Yes."

I couldn't believe they were talking about Joey's funeral. I wanted to press my hands to my ears to stifle the words, to scream so loud I would drown out the new reality that had taken over my life. But I knew I had to keep it together. At least until I was alone in my closet with Joey's sweatshirt pressed against my mouth, muffling my sobs.

"We've asked the baseball team to serve as pallbearers," Mrs. Walther said. "And we'd like you all to sit up front with us. I was thinking that you could maybe choose something to read. As a group. Or however you think would be—" She bowed her head then, squeezing her eyes shut, and her body began to shake. Mr. Walther moved toward his wife, rubbing her shoulders.

"We thought you might like to make a few CDs for the viewing, too," Mr. Walther said. "I'm sure you'd know better than us what—"

"There's going to be a viewing?" I asked, my body stiff.

Mrs. Walther sniffled. "We thought it was important."

"Oh," I said, squeezing my hands tight. The thought of seeing my boyfriend's body laid out in a coffin made me feel like I was going to throw up. But the question that came next made me feel worse. Two words strung together on a rushed and frantic wave.

"What happened?" Joey's mother asked, her eyes trained on me.

"Trisha," Mr. Walther said. "We decided we weren't going to—"

"I know Joey is . . . *was* wild, and beautifully fearless. I'm not blaming anyone. And I'm so grateful that he wasn't alone, that your faces were the last ones he saw. But I *need* to understand," Mrs. Walther said, fisting her hands tight. *"What happened Saturday?"*

My heart exploded in my chest, every breath so tight I felt like I might pass out.

"I explained to you this afternoon," Adam said, "Maggie doesn't remember anything after climbing up the trail with Joey."

I looked at Adam, barely registering that he had been to speak with them already. That he'd talked to them about me.

"Maggie," Mrs. Walther said, "can't you tell me anything?"

My throat threatened to close up on me. It was the guilt of not remembering, of surviving when Joey hadn't. But I forced the words out. "I'm trying to see it, to remember, but—"

"You were with him, though? At the top?"

I closed my eyes, wanting to go back instead of facing what lay ahead, and saw the treetops, sweeping slowly from side to side. Then my eyes traveled down the length of several thick trunks, resting on my friends as they stood expectantly along the bank of the swimming hole.

Don't stand there looking down for too long, Adam called.

My eyes popped open. Found Adam. He leaned forward in his seat, staring right back at me.

"Adam told me not to look down for too long," I said. That part had to be right. It was like a movie playing on some invisible screen, the way I could see his face, tipped up toward me, how I could hear his voice echoing off the walls of the gorge.

"Yeah," Adam whispered. "I did."

"Wait," Shannon said, her eyes flickering from me to Adam and back again. "You remember something? Something new?"

I stared at her, watching her long eyelashes beat time with the second hand of the clock on the mantle, taking in the way her hair had gone stringy from not being washed, following the curve of her neck turning into her shoulder and sweeping down her tanned arm. And then I got another flash.

Tanna smacking Shannon's arm. The spark of a smirk on Shannon's face.

My voice, one word: *Bitch.*

And Joey's: *Part of what we love about her.*

The sounds echo-echo-echoed off the stone walls of my skull.

Still staring. Shannon's brown eyes, the smooth peachy skin of her cheeks, the strawberry pink of her lips.

"Maggie?" Tanna said, her voice tight, high-pitched. "Are you okay?"

"No, I—" I tried to steady my rushed breathing, knowing I had to lie. These new flashes, I needed to figure out how to find more, how to piece together the whole scene before I said anything. "I'm sorry. I don't remember anything new. Just walking up to the top. Standing there." I looked to Mrs. Walther, tears spilling from my eyes. "I don't know what happened. I wish I could tell you. But it's just . . . gone."

Adam stood from his chair, and everyone turned to look at him. I wanted to take the chance to sneak away, to duck into one of those photographs and slip right back into the past.

"I think he was trying one of his stupid stunts," Adam said, leaning down and plucking a few pictures from the pile, shuffling through them.

"He was always so crazy up there." Pete rubbed a hand on my knee, squeezing in a way that let me know they all had my back. Which was good, because I didn't think I could face any more questions. "At one point or another, I think we all told him to chill."

"Joey?" Rylan asked. "Chill? You think he even knew the definition of that word?"

Pete and Adam chuckled. From her spot on the floor, Tanna scooted closer to me, her warm eyes meeting mine as she stopped near my feet, her body shielding my own. And Shannon, she slumped beside me, practically melting into the cushions of the couch.

"We were told that he hit his head," Mr. Walther said.

"And that you all went into the water to pull him to shore."

"Except Shannon," Pete said. "She went for the phone."

"I knew it was bad," Shannon whispered, "when he didn't pop up from the water and crack some stupid joke."

"And he was still breathing?" Mr. Walther asked.

"It was strained." Tanna pressed a hand to her chest and took a deep breath. Then reached out to me, wrapped her fingers around my ankle.

"I didn't know that," I said, my chest feeling like it was caving in. I looked at everyone in the room, my eyes stopping on Shannon. "No one told me anything about him breathing. He was alive?"

"When they got him to the towel, he looked up at me." Shannon closed her eyes. Her whole face pulled tight. "I know he saw me. He tried to say something. But I couldn't make it out. And then he squeezed my hand once." Shannon's voice broke open. With all the passion that I had ever felt in my life, I hated that the memory of Joey's last moments were hers instead of mine.

"We started CPR," Adam said, "when Shan noticed he wasn't breathing anymore."

The room fell silent. It felt like a fog had fallen over us, trailing into our mouths so no more words could be spoken. I heard Shannon's soft, breathy cries. All I could think was that while I was glad Joey had someone with him in his last minutes, I despised that it wasn't me. For a moment, all that deep, dark hate was directed at her. And then I felt horrible. She'd lost Joey, too. We all had. So I pulled her against me, rubbed her back, and felt myself begin to suffocate under the weight of our sadness. Looking at the letters of Joey's name stitched on his baseball shirt, I tried not to think about how Shannon's breath, and perfume, and tears were evaporating the last scents Joey had left on the fabric enfolding me.

I tried not to think about Joey's parents, who were still on the floor, deflated and broken. I thought it was over then. But they had one more question. The one that I'd been asking myself since the police station.

"Where was Joey Friday night?" Mrs. Walther paused. "He told us he was staying at Adam's house."

"Wait, he didn't?" Shannon asked, pulling away from me. "Joey took us home—Maggie and me and Pete. Adam called right after we dropped Maggie off. I just thought . . ."

"Nope," Adam said, shaking his head. "I talked to him sometime after twelve, but that's it."

"None of you have any ideas?" Mrs. Walther asked.

We looked around at one another, shaking our heads. It seemed like a totally insignificant detail when you considered the whole mess, but it hit hard in that moment. We might not ever know where Joey went after Jimmy Dutton's party. Joey wasn't there to tell us anymore.

His room felt like a bubble. A safe place that, when I closed my eyes, gave me the illusion that Joey was still alive. The air practically sizzled with his energy, so intense I could have believed he was standing next to me. I wasn't supposed to touch anything. I'd promised I wouldn't when I made my escape, using the excuse that I wanted to grab a few of his CDs for the mix we were going to make. But I had to.

I leaned down and pressed my face into his pillow, breathing him in. Imagined him lying there, perfectly alive. Then I crossed the room and opened his closet door as quietly as I could, running my fingers along the soft fabric of his clothes. I wished I could tuck myself into the thick shadows of the small space. To stay there for the rest of my life.

But nothing that I wanted could happen anymore.

So I reached for the inside handle of the closet door and started to swing it shut. But my fingers brushed against something wrapped around the neck of the silver knob, stopping me.

I looked down. Smiled.

There, twisted and pulled tight, was a rainbow-colored necklace, a pattern of tiny beaded flowers. Pete had won it for me at the Spring Carnival, just five weeks ago. Joey couldn't come because his father had scored some killer tickets for a Reds game in Cincinnati. Joey had been excited for the game, but he'd been pissed we were all doing something without him. He'd always hated missing out.

After the carnival, Tanna drove me home, both of us singing to loud music as the wind rushed at us through the open windows of her car. I'd been wishing Joey would call me; I wanted to hear the velvety tone of his voice before I slipped under my covers and fell asleep. But he'd been so late, I didn't talk to him until the next day. When he stopped by my house, we went up to my room, and I'd flung the necklace in the air, teasing him that another guy had given me jewelry. He'd better be careful or someone might just steal me away. And then I shoved the bright flowers into the right-hand side of my dresser drawer, along with a messy collection of barrettes and bottles of nail polish, with Joey leaning into me, tugging at the waist of my shirt and whispering that he was the only one for me. I'd had no idea he'd taken the silly necklace, but somehow seeing it wrapped around the handle of his closet door, knowing he'd thought of me every time he'd seen it, made me happy.

I grabbed a stack of CDs from his dresser before making my way out into the darkened hallway. As I stepped to the top of the staircase, I was thinking that I would give anything for one more night with Joey, so I could tell him and show him and make him feel exactly how much he meant to me.

I was three or four steps down before I heard them. Hushed whispers, hurried and insistent. The first voice was Shannon's. The second, Adam's. The sharpness that punctuated the tone of the conversation stopped me. My hand gripped the railing and held tight.

"Adam, that's not fair. You have to think about—"

"It's *all* I'm thinking about, Shannon."

"Then you should understand that we can't—"

"No. You need to understand. I'm not going to do this. I won't."

"Is this about that phone call? The night of Dutton's party?"

"That's none of your business, Shannon."

"The hell it isn't. I know you were fighting. You have to tell me what—"

"The only thing I have to do right now is leave." Adam sounded so angry, nothing like himself. And that scared me. "I can't handle this. Not for one more second."

There were footsteps then. And the click of the front door.

I rushed down, my palm sliding across the railing, just in time to see Adam step through the open doorway. Shannon's back was to me, her body tense.

"She's right, Adam," I whispered.

Adam stopped. Stood there for a moment. And then turned to face me, tears welling in his red-rimmed eyes.

Shannon turned, too, her tears spilling over, running down her cheeks and dripping off her chin.

"Right about what?" Adam asked, his tone softening a bit.

"You can't just leave. We have to do this together."

Adam bit his lower lip and looked around the entry. "It's just too much," he said, tipping his head toward those black Converse shoes. "Being here. Doing this."

"This isn't about us," I said. "It's about Joey. And his family. It sucks and hurts and we hate it, but we're doing this because we love him." I wondered how I could feel so comfortable telling Adam that I loved Joey when I'd never had the guts to tell Joey himself. I felt like screaming, knowing I'd lost the chance, that I'd never have it again.

Adam shook his head.

"Shan said you and Joey were fighting?" I was dying to ask a thousand questions at once but forced myself to let them go until Adam and I were alone and he might actually tell me something. "Is that why you're so—"

"Nothing was going on." Adam looked at Shannon. Then me. "It was stupid."

Shannon reached out toward Adam, but he pulled away.

"He was a brother to you," Shannon said. "He wasn't perfect. He was more than a little crazy sometimes, but that's why we loved him. Right?"

Adam pressed his hands to his face. Sighed. "Right. It's just that . . . He *died*. And I'm so freaking pissed off, I swear I'd punch him in the face if he were standing right here."

"That's normal, right? I mean, I feel that way, too, sometimes," I said, trying to smile. "And then the next second, I'm a slobbering mess, just wanting to give him one more hug."

"We've all turned schizophrenic," Shannon said with a snort. "Joey would be proud he's had that effect on us."

Adam shook his head. "The sick thing is that you're right."

"So, you're staying?" I asked.

Adam closed the door, shutting out the dark night. "Yeah," he said. "I guess I don't have a choice."

"Thank you," Shannon said.

Adam looked at her, something unfamiliar crossing over his face, sending a ripple of fear through my chest. I tried to push the thought away, but it kept coming back. Adam seemed different somehow. A shade darker. And I was suddenly afraid that Joey, and all those memories, weren't the only things I'd lost at the cliff top.

6

A Punched-up Shade of Blue

It had hit me the night before, after coming home from Joey's house. The memory crashed into me as I was falling asleep, and I couldn't get it out of my mind. The image of Joey lying on the ground. Unmoving.

It's like my brain had taken a snapshot of the moment and seared the single frame to the insides of my eyelids so that every few seconds it would wash over me again. Pull me under. Drown me. Joey on the bank—just lying there—his legs bent awkwardly, head tipped back, mouth gaping open.

I squeezed my eyes tight and pressed my fingertips into the lids, turning the flash into a million pinpricks of light— erasing his death.

The vision made me feel this desperate need to hide in the vacuum of my closet. But I wasn't alone. And I didn't want anyone to know that I'd started to spend so much time backed into a corner, huddled beneath my clothes. So I stayed where I was, burrowed between Tanna and Shannon.

Earlier, when we'd finished the last of Joey's posters and CDs, after Pete left us sitting on my front lawn with the setting sun turning the sky a bruised shade of purplish blue, Tanna had insisted on spending the night, saying we should use pillows and blankets to make a bed on the floor of my room, like we used to do when we were kids. With only one day until the funeral, Shannon had agreed, saying that none of us should be alone.

I didn't tell her that, for me, *alone* was the only thing that felt right anymore.

Lying on the floor, digging my toes into the carpet to give myself the reassurance that something beneath me was solid, I lied to myself. Told myself Joey had just been sleeping. Because that was easier. An escape. Lying took me to the times that were protected, indestructible.

Like the semester of freshman health class, when Joey and I would shuffle to the back of the classroom, duck behind Chris Grater's wiry Afro, and whisper back and forth until the interminable video of the day began. Then we'd nestle down in our seats, prop our heads on bunched-up fleece jackets, and close our eyes. I always opened mine again, watching Joey for a few minutes as the drone of the documentary voice-over began, counting the freckles dotting the slope of his nose, or thinking about braiding his chocolate-brown hair, imagining the feel of the silky strands sliding against the length of my fingers until the information about STDs or news of the latest supervirus trickled into my brain and I was swept away by the sleep that had overtaken Joey.

Just sleeping, I told myself, pressing my shoulders, my

back, my butt against the bedroom floor—against solid ground. Pressing my mind forward, tripping away from that horrible vision, and onto the next. Adam's face, his eyes, stricken with panic. But that only made me feel more alone. More unsteady and in need of balance. Why was everything making me feel like I was suspended in eternal free fall?

"You guys checked your phones again, right?" I asked the darkness, the steady sound of sleepy breathing coming from both of my friends. "When we turned off the light?"

"Yeah." Tanna flipped to her side, facing me. I could smell the soapy scent of the Noxzema she'd slathered on her face earlier. "I did."

"Me, too." Shannon tossed an arm up and over her head.

"Nothing?" I asked.

"Nada," Shannon said. "It's official. Adam's ignoring us."

"I don't get it," I said. "Why wouldn't he show tonight? How could he miss helping with the posters and CDs for the funeral?"

"The important thing is that we know he's okay. I talked to his mom earlier today, remember?" Tanna reached out and gave my hand a squeeze. "We're all having trouble with this, and we won't all deal with it in the same way."

"Yeah, but he's, like, completely shut us out," I said. "How many times did you text him?"

"Not as many as you," Shannon said with a yawn.

"I sent him *three* nine-one-one messages. And left him, like, a thousand voice mails." I flipped to my stomach, grabbing my phone and pressing the button to take it out of sleep mode.

"Maybe he just needs a little time," Tanna said. "To process—"

"Nothing," I said, scrolling through my texts. "Still nothing." Somehow, Adam's absence was making me feel twice as empty. Which didn't make any sense. I knew he was alive. He was out there, somewhere. And that should have made me feel relieved. But instead, his sudden disappearance left me twice as shaky, twice as unsure about the world that was suddenly closing in around me.

"Where do you guys think he is?" Shannon asked, her voice trailing into the darkness, tripping across Tanna and me.

"Hell if I know," I said, tossing my phone on the floor near my pillow, close enough for me to grab in a flash if Adam finally decided to respond. "All we know for sure is what Pete said after he left here and drove past Adam's house—that his car wasn't in the driveway. Trust me, if I knew where to go, I'd leave right now and ream him for ignoring us."

"I meant *Joey*," Shannon said, her soft words tumbling after mine. There was a pause then, a silence that seeped into our bones as the truth of Joey's death washed over us again. "I keep thinking he's on the moon. I've been picturing him up there in that purplish-white glow. I see him watching us. Listening in."

My chest tightened with the thought of him being so very far away. I bit at my lip, trying to keep all sound trapped inside.

"I see him in a field," Tanna said. "The grass practically glows, it's so green, and the sky above him is this punched-up shade of blue. He's running, his arms pumping with his steps. And he looks strong. Healthy. But most important, he's smiling."

I was jealous and ashamed, and I didn't want to tell them that my vision of Joey was so unlike theirs. That what I mostly saw was him lying on the ground at the Jumping Hole. Dead. Where he was now, that was something I hadn't yet dared to face. And I didn't want to. So I said the first thing that came to my mind, needing to escape before I became locked in the grip of yet something else that would drown me.

"I just want to rewind everything," I said. "To take it all back."

"Take what back?" Tanna's voice was stronger, more awake.

"*Everything!* Planning the day at the gorge, driving with you guys instead of Joey, taking that stupid dare. What if one small thing changed? Would we all be hanging out right now, listening to music while Joey laughed at something stupid someone said, instead of making posters and planning the music for his—"

"Maggie," Tanna said, "you can't do that."

"But I can't stop myself." I sat up and pulled my knees to my chest. "What if it's as simple as one moment? One tiny thing, like that kiss on the rocks? What if I'd kissed him a little longer? Would he be alive right now? Or what if I'd stayed with him Friday night, what if I'd been with him . . . wherever he was?"

"You've got to let that go," Shannon said. "It's going to drive you crazy. And none of us know, so—"

"Besides," Tanna's hand fluttered against my back, her fingers pressing into the cotton of my shirt, "it doesn't work like that."

"And then I think all kinds of stupid shit, right? Like, what if I'd just had sex with him at prom? Could something as far back as a few weeks ago have made a difference?"

"No way, Mags." Tanna's voice was a whisper. Like she wasn't sure if she was right or not.

"But if we'd done it that night, like he'd wanted to, instead of me holding out for the week his parents were going out of town . . . If I hadn't been so against becoming a total cliché, he wouldn't have died a virgin."

"Oh, God, Maggie, you think . . ." Shannon's voice fell, dropped away with her thought. Then it came back, even stronger. "You can't blame yourself for anything like that."

"Who else is to blame?" My question strung out in the air between us like a thread, ready to break.

Tanna and Shannon were silent in the darkness.

"No one." I tipped my forehead against my knees and tried to hold back my tears.

"Maggie," Tanna said, rubbing my back in slow circles. "You have to stop this."

I choked on a sob, then let it all the way out. Sitting there between them, clutching tight to the edge of my blanket, watching the clock tick me from the-first-Tuesday-without-Joey into the-first-Wednesday-without-Joey, I needed an escape.

So I focused on the calming memories of what had been, scrolling through the years, the stages, the people we once were and had come to be.

But somehow, that made everything feel worse.

"I'm just really tired," I said. "I don't want to talk anymore."

"Are you sure?" Tanna asked, her hand slipping away from my back.

"Yeah," I said, the word shaking out into the darkness. "Please."

I lay back then, closed my eyes, and did the one thing that always helped me when I was feeling alone.

I remembered my favorite night with Joey.

The most important night of all.

The night *we* became *us*.

I'd always loved the sky. The night sky, though, was the best. The purplish-blue blanket that folded itself over my little town, it promised me things. Whispered to me when I was in that hazy state of almost sleep where anything seemed possible.

Like Joey and me.

Together.

After so many years of my secret longing, it was fitting that it all started under the veiled and sparkling shelter only a night sky could offer.

"Favorite midnight snack?" Joey lay next to me in the bed of his new black truck, which was actually used, his shoulder bumping mine as we played Twenty Questions in the middle of an abandoned back field on the outskirts of town.

"Bozie's Donuts."

Joey's head tipped toward me, his hair falling across his forehead. "No way."

I smiled and bit my lower lip to keep myself from looking as excited as I felt to be so close to him. He smelled good. Like cut grass and honeysuckle. And I wanted to taste him.

"I mean, *seriously*, no way." As Joey shook his head, his eyes remained plastered to mine. "That's too creepy."

"Last time I checked, there's nothing creepy about Bozie's Donuts."

Joey chuckled. "Wait'll you see this."

He sat up and slid across the open tailgate of his truck, disappearing in the thick blackness that blanketed the night around us. I readjusted myself on the inflatable camping mattress Joey had unrolled in the truck's bed and scooted closer to the center, listening to the sound of Joey's footsteps as they mingled with the crooning chirp of the crickets. He got into the truck, and I heard rustling, then the soft sound of music before the slam of his driver's side door rippled across the open field. He hopped into the truck's bed, a white bag swinging in his hand.

"Check it out." He held the bag in the air.

I laughed, surprised to see the Bozie's Donuts logo. "That is a little creepy."

"I thought we'd get hungry while we waited." Joey opened the bag and took a deep whiff.

"You ever gonna tell me what we're waiting for?" I raised myself on my elbows, feeling the shiver of my hair against my neck.

"It's a surprise." Joey held the bag toward me. "You like devil's food?"

"Are you kidding?" I sat up and reached into the bag, feeling my way around some frosted donuts and a twisted pretzel donut before finally finding the perfect specimen. "They're only the best."

"Creepy."

I laughed, wishing he would sit right next to me again. That he would lie down, turn to me, and flip this thing between us into full speed.

After taking a few bites of the sweet donut, I looked at Joey. He tipped his head back, staring up at the sky as he wiped crumbs off his hands and swallowed his last bite.

"You have to give me a hint." I decided to lie down again, hoping the action would lure him closer. "Is everyone meeting us out here? Is that what we're waiting on?"

"Nope." Joey slid toward me. "Tonight's just for you and me."

I smiled. Then pinched my lips together. Tight. It had been awkward, this thing between us. Whatever *it* was. Joey and I had hung out alone a zillion times. I mean, we'd grown up together, the six of us, and we'd all spent time in small groups or pairs while the others were busy. But when Joey had stopped me after school exactly one week earlier and said he had a surprise planned, that he wanted me to be his first passenger after passing his driving test, he was nervous. And *nothing* made Joey nervous. I knew from the way his voice wavered, how his eyes looked everywhere but right into mine. And that had gotten me excited. I'd never told anyone about my long-standing, secret crush on

Joey. Ever. Because I knew what feelings like mine could do to a friendship. And I couldn't lose him.

"Joey, look!" I flung my hand into the air, pointing at a brilliant trail of light streaking across the sky.

"There we go," he said, lying down and scooting his body right up against mine.

"Should we make a wish?" I stared at the fading light. "Shooting star, and all?"

Joey's hand reached out, his fingers twining into mine. "We're going to have plenty of wishes to make tonight."

As soon as he spoke, another star flashed across the sky. "Did you see that?"

"It's a meteor shower," Joey said. "And the show is just starting."

"No way!" I wiggled a little with my excitement, causing the truck to sway beneath us. "I've never seen a meteor shower. I've always wanted to."

"Same here," Joey said. "I thought it would be the perfect way to show you . . . well, how I'm feeling."

I turned toward him, but not all the way. You never want to go all the way. "How you're feeling?"

Joey rolled his eyes. "You really gonna make me work for it?"

"I just want to hear you say it."

"I'm having feelings. Different than normal." Joey traced his thumb along my lower lip. "For you."

"Good feelings?" I licked my lips, tasting the sugary coating left over from my donut. The song on the stereo changed, and I recognized the beginning beats of the Dave Matthews Band's "You and Me."

Joey leaned forward, his breath a sweet, delicious heat that had me spinning under another leaping star.

"Definitely." His voice was a whisper, but it washed through me.

And then he kissed me.

It was insistent from the beginning. That kiss, there was nothing soft about it. Like he'd been waiting his whole life to finally make it happen. And it swept me away, carried me further than anything ever had. I rode the wave as long as I could, feeling his fingers twisting through my hair, the way his body pressed against mine, how his eyelashes brushed against the upper part of my cheek. I'm not sure how long it lasted, our first kiss. All I know is that it was long enough to flip the earth inside out. To turn everything around forever. I no longer cared about the beauty of the plunging stars. All I wanted was to kiss him again. And again. And again.

Joey stopped before I was even close to ready. All kinds of things raced through my mind—*Did the kiss not measure up? Did his feelings vanish as quickly as they had appeared?*—until he smiled, his fingers stroking my chin, trailing slowly down my neck, lighting my entire body on fire.

"That was nice," he said.

I nodded, unable to find my voice.

"I want to gulp you down."

I loved the smoky sound of his voice as he whispered to me.

"But I have to take sips. Or else this thing could be dangerous."

I took a deep breath. And I finally understood. He felt

the same way I did. And everything was going to be fine. Slow. But good. I could handle that.

After bumping his nose against mine and giving me one last small kiss, he looked up. I tipped my forehead against his and stared at the dancing sky.

I wanted the night to last forever. It killed me, knowing that each moment ticked me closer to the time we would have to part from the magic of the field. I looked at Joey, traced the dip of his nose with my eyes. And I got an idea.

"You have to be quiet," I said as I pulled my phone from my pocket.

"Why?" Joey looked at me with curious eyes.

I had already punched in the number and was listening to the third ring. "Shh."

"Honey, what is it? Are you okay?" My mom's voice was heavy, and I knew that I'd woken her. I wondered if she was in bed or still on the couch with the quilt draped over her legs while late night television flickered light across the living room.

"I'm fine, Mom," I said with a yawn. "Just tired. Is it okay if I sleep over at Tanna's tonight?"

My mom caught my yawn. "That's fine," she said. "Just call me in the morning."

"Okay." I grinned at Joey. "'Night."

When I closed my phone and slid it back into my pocket, Joey turned to his side, propping himself on an elbow. "You," he said, "are trouble."

I laughed, the sound of my voice skipping across the empty field. "You gonna call home, too?" My heart was beating fast, in time with the rapid melody of the crickets that surrounded us. I wasn't sure what Joey would think about what I'd just done. I knew that call had been the final step, crossing a line that meant our friendship was now something much more complicated. And I was excited to see what lay ahead. "Or do I have to spend a night in this field *alone*?"

Joey leaned forward, his lips brushing mine, lingering, his breath an intoxicating sugary mist. "You think I'd miss out on this opportunity?" Joey asked, shaking his head. "Not. On. Your. Life."

7

Crashing Onto Me

I held my breath because of the smell. It was stale, and musty, and wrong.

My feet stepped slowly, skidding every so often on the thick carpet, a deep maroon pool that sucked me under with its circular pattern, pulling me forward to the last place I ever wanted to be. The last place I ever thought I would be.

"There she is," someone just ahead of me whispered.

I did not look up.

"Do you think it's true?" another voice asked.

Shannon's grasp on my hand tightened. "Ignore them."

"You got this," Tanna said. I wasn't sure if she was speaking to herself or to me.

The dark box was just ahead, its shiny surface glinting, even in the dim lighting of the room. One glance and I squeezed my eyes so tight I saw starbursts. I wished I could squeeze so hard I'd pass out and miss this entire thing.

The faint sound of "You and Me" by the Dave Matthews

Band caught in my ears. At first, I thought I had imagined it. But then I remembered the CDs Pete, Tanna, Shannon, and I had made. I could hardly recall sitting on my front lawn as we made the playlists on Pete's iPod, or going inside to burn the songs to disks. What I remembered most was all of us wondering why Adam had refused to join, worrying about why he was pulling away, and hoping that we would get him back.

When I opened my eyes, I saw it again. The long box. But I saw something else, too. Joey's profile peeking just above the side. It looked like he was sleeping.

Those long-ago memories rushed me again. Joey in health class. Joey lying under the shooting stars. Joey—just sleeping.

But then my eyes skittered around the room, and all illusion vanished.

The terrible sadness that had overtaken me, the truth of Joey's death, shadowed everyone in darkness. I looked at the crowd of varsity cheerleaders, sports lovers, drama clubbers, and overall party freaks hovering around the pocket of easels on the right side of the church, their backs facing the hundreds of pictures we'd taped to the poster boards. It felt as if each person in the room was staring directly at me. Then my eyes jumped left, found Joey's baseball team clamoring around a seating area, all in white Oxford shirts and black ties, their faces so melted by sadness I could hardly recognize them as they waited for me to break open.

I bobbed through the center aisle of the church, Tanna and Shannon at my sides, focusing on one thing: Joey's mother's shoes. They were tan, flat, and ugly. *Joey would be so embarrassed,* I thought, then scolded myself. The poor woman had just lost her son. It was a wonder she had found the sanity to put on any shoes at all.

Five steps later, I was in front of her, standing on two shaky legs. I put my hand on her shoulder and kissed her soppy cheek, trying to keep my eyes from darting to the body lying next to her husband. As I moved away from Mrs. Walther, Joey's father reached out and folded me against him. He whispered something across the top of my head, but all I caught was the vibration coming from his chest. I wanted to stop time, to stay there in his arms forever, because his shirt smelled like Joey. And he was the last stop before my final good-bye.

Mr. Walther pulled away from me, holding me at arm's length as his eyes wandered the planes of my face. "Doesn't he look peaceful?" Mr. Walther asked, tilting his head.

And I turned.

Faced him for the last time.

My Joey.

Tanna uncurled my fingers from the side of the coffin and tucked my hand into hers, squeezing. "It's okay," she said. "Just say good-bye."

I sucked in a deep breath and looked from Joey's cheeks to his nose to his chin, wanting with everything I was to see one more radiant smile light up his face. Wanting to see his eyes flash out at the world around him.

His blue, blue eyes. They matched his favorite T-shirt almost perfectly. I was glad Rylan had talked his parents out of burying Joey in a suit; I knew they'd had several arguments over the matter. Rylan had insisted on Joey's sky blue, HullabaLOU T-shirt, which he had picked up last summer when the six of us spent the entire day at the music festival. It was crisp and pulled tight across Joey's still chest and was actually tucked into his favorite Abercrombie jeans, which was so not how he did things, but whatever. At least he would be comfortable.

"How'm I supposed to say good-bye?" I asked.

"You just do it," Shannon said. "You gotta."

I shook my head. Tears fell from my chin onto Joey's face. I wanted to wipe them away. But I was afraid to touch him.

Terrified.

And that nearly made me collapse. Because *this* was Joey.

"Okay," I said. "I can do this."

"Yeah," Shannon said. "You can."

I nodded. More tears fell.

"Do you want us to stay?" Tanna asked. "Or leave you alone?"

I didn't know how to answer. And then I forgot the question, because I heard him. *Right* behind me. A huge wave of relief surged through me as I turned, a smile daring to form on my lips, and said his name.

"Joey?" It's crazy, I know, but I really believed. The waxy version of him lying so still did *not* seem real, so it felt right, the hope that blossomed through my chest.

But then his mother crumpled in her chair, and I realized my mistake.

It wasn't him at all. No. It had been Rylan.

"Oh, God," I said, my hand slamming to my mouth.

Rylan looked at me, his blue eyes pinched tight, and blew a burst of air from his lips.

"I'm sorry," I whispered.

Rylan's shoulders slumped as he slid into the chair next to his mother. He leaned forward, propping his elbows on his knees, and buried his face in his hands. It was the first moment I wondered what it might be like to live in the Walthers' house, so quiet with Joey gone. It must be so much harder for Rylan to be left behind, a reminder to everyone just by being himself, because he looked and sounded *so* much like Joey.

I turned then, back to my good-bye, and leaned toward Joey's still face.

My lips were so close to his ear that I would have felt the heat of him if he'd been alive.

"I love you, Joey," I whispered for the first and last time in my life.

Then I pressed two fingers to my mouth, placing my final kiss for him there, and settled my fingers on his lips.

But his lips were all wrong.

They were cold and hard. The exact way I did *not* want to remember Joey.

The moment the touch registered in my brain, I realized that I never should have done it. The seconds my fingers rested on his stony lips would never be erased. Not in all my life. No matter what I did to scrape them away.

I turned and ran then, through the throngs of hushed people trying not to stare, past my mother, who had held out her arms to stop me. I shoved myself through the back door of the church and out into the bright light of the last May of Joey's life.

My knees dug into the soft soil, the grass prickling my skin.

My body heaved, stomach tight as I threw up a wave of acidic bile, the only thing left in me.

I curled my fingers into the ground, ripping up a handful of the earth beneath me, hurling it into the bushes that lined the side of the church.

Tanna's feet, her black-polished toes and black strappy sandals, appeared at my side. "You okay?"

"No." If I'd had the energy, I would have screamed it loud enough for everyone in the world to hear.

Tanna knelt beside me, gently pulling my hair out of my face, tugging it into a ponytail, and securing it with an elastic band.

"I want to be alone." I curled into myself, a tight ball, and rested my cheek on the cool grass, closing my eyes and feeling a ghostly breeze attempt to dry the tears on my cheeks.

"Your mom was chasing after you," Tanna said. "I convinced her to let me come out instead. You sure you want me to go?"

I nodded, the fresh scent of cut grass mingling with the sour smell of my vomit. "Just tell her I need some space."

"Pete and Adam are over by the koi pond," Tanna said. "I'm going to tell them to wait for you."

I didn't say anything. Just focused on my breathing.

Tanna rubbed her fingernails along my back, giving me goose bumps. "You're still alive, Mags. You might not feel like it. But you have to keep going."

"I love you, Tan, but I need you to leave," I said. "Please."

"You have all of us here to help you through this," Tanna said. "When you're ready. Don't forget that."

She stood then, without another word, and walked away. When the vibration of her footsteps stopped buzzing the ground beneath me, I turned onto my back and stared up at the too-bright, too-blue sky, wishing it would come crashing down onto me.

"What're you playing?" I asked as I sat on the large rock between Pete and Adam. When Tanna left me, I had planned to lie there in the grass until my body failed and I no longer had to force myself to remember to breathe. But then I thought of the shrink they were making me see next week and imagined myself being wheeled down a dim corridor in some far-off mental hospital. I couldn't lose it completely. At least not in a way that was so obvious to others.

Pete's fingers kept moving, plucking invisible strings on the imaginary guitar propped on his lap. He did it often, the whole air guitar thing. Especially when he was bored or angry. Once I'd even caught his fingers playing after he fell asleep during a movie.

"Skynard," he said. "'Freebird.'"

I stretched my legs forward, kicking out of the high-heeled sandals Tanna had yanked from my closet the night before. "It should be raining," I said, tipping my face to the clear blue sky. "Angry, thrashing rain with streaks of lightning and crashing thunder."

Adam looked up, too, squinting at the sun. "That would make more sense."

"It should rain forever," I said. "Now that we're stuck without him."

Pete rocked forward a bit, looking down at the koi swimming in the little rock-lined pond. "Sucks inside," he said. "Hard. We had to get away."

I stared into the glimmering water, focusing on the largest fish in the group. It was silver and black and almost disappeared as it whipped around the others, a streak of shimmering lightning. It seemed like everything I saw or thought of brought me right back to Joey. The fish was no exception with its fearless, unstoppable energy.

"I think he looks good," Pete said, tilting his face toward me without looking into my eyes.

"You do?" I asked, my voice shaking.

"Not really." Pete scrunched his eyes, like he was in pain just thinking about Joey lying there in his coffin. "They did a good job on his head, where he hit the ledge, which is surprising. Other than that, he looks like some kind of wax version of himself. But I wasn't about to say that to *you*."

"You just did." I chuckled. The sound felt scratchy and raw as it traveled up my throat. "And I agree." My fingers were still tingling from the icy feel of Joey's lips. I wondered if I would go through the rest of my life with my skin crawling as if I was still touching his death.

"I'm just glad they put him in that HullabaLOU T-shirt." Adam's voice was small, like he was very far away.

I sucked in a deep breath, remembering our day at the crazy-huge music festival. Pete had scored us the tickets through someone his dad knew, and all six of us had spent ten hours in the crowd, sweating in the summer sun, drinking what we could get our hands on, and dancing to the coolest bands. It was almost dark when the Steve Miller Band hit the main stage, and the rain began to fall. It came in a huge rush, like the clouds above knew how hot and sticky we were, and drenched us in an instant. The six of us danced, and laughed, and sang all at the same time, spinning on the slippery, muddy ground. It was at the very end of "Fly Like an Eagle," when they were singing about time slippin' forward, that Joey swept me against his body and pressed his lips to my neck. "This is the best night of my life," he'd said with a laugh. "And you're the best thing that's ever happened to me."

It was the closest Joey had ever come to telling me that he loved me. Then he spun me away and whipped his hands into the air, bumping into Adam and Pete as they pulled Tanna up from the muddy ground. Shannon slung an arm around my shoulders and sang along with the band, droplets of water rushing down her face, drip-drip-dripping off the wavy strands of her darkened hair.

If only we could go back. When Joey leaned in, his warm breath tickling my neck, that would be the one moment of my life I'd choose to relive. Over, and over, and over again.

"You guys want to get together later?" Pete asked, his voice low, like he knew he was pushing when he wasn't sure if he should. "Hang out and . . . I don't know, just be together or something? All of us? I feel like he'd like that. Joey, I mean."

I looked at Adam, the way his eyes had fallen down to the ground, not looking at either of us, not responding at all.

"Yeah," I said. "We should. Adam, you in?"

"I don't know," Adam said. "My mom's kind of clingy right now, you know? And I have some shit for school—"

"Dude," Pete said. "School? What about *Joey*?"

Adam looked up then, his eyes flaring. "Just call me when you figure it out. I'll come if I can."

"Right," Pete said, standing. "I gotta go in. My parents should be here by now."

"We'll be there in a few," I said, looking at Adam, wondering how the person sitting beside me was the same guy I'd considered one of my best friends for most of my life. Because, suddenly, he seemed like someone I barely knew. I was dying to touch him, to feel that he wasn't so far away. I missed him like crazy, had thought of a thousand things I'd wanted to say to him over the last few days while he ignored us, but I didn't know how to cross the expanse that all the questions had created between us.

Pete walked away, and I tried to think of the right way to start. Of how I could get the answers I needed without pushing Adam into an even darker place.

"I've tried calling you," I said, deciding to talk to him

as if nothing had changed, saying exactly what was on my mind instead of dancing around all the feelings. "Like, a hundred times."

Adam nodded. "Haven't felt much like talking."

"You can't push us all away, Adam. We're still here."

Adam buried his face in his hands. "I know."

"I don't want to make things worse. But there's stuff I need to ask."

Adam sighed. "Like?"

"Why were you and Joey fighting?" The question tumbled out before I could stop it. I knew it was the wrong way to approach this new version of Adam, but I didn't take it back. I just stared at the glinting back of the silver fish, hoping it was the moment I would finally get some answers.

"I already told you." Adam's voice was tinged with a shaky kind of anger. "It was nothing."

I closed my eyes and pictured Joey at the party standing on Jimmy Dutton's back deck, a wave of something powerful rolling off him and dashing across the lawn, right toward Adam. But I'd been standing there, too. Right next to Adam. A little more than drunk, my head spinning from dancing in circles. And I couldn't be sure some of that anger hadn't been directed at me. If that's why Joey hadn't told me where he'd spent Friday night.

"I don't believe that it was nothing." I swiped a few strands of hair from my eyes. "When I think back to Dutton's party, the part where Joey came outside and first saw that you were there, something seemed off. Like, really off. I want to know what was going on."

Adam stared off to the batch of trees that separated the back area of the church from a line of houses that had been converted into a dentist's office, an insurance agency, and a picture-framing store.

"It's complicated." Adam clasped his hands together.

"Was he mad at me?" I asked. "Did he say anything about me that night, when you called him after the party?"

"Maggie," Adam said, turning to look at me. "What reason could Joey possibly have had to be angry with you?"

I shrugged. Felt tears welling up in my eyes. "I don't know. But everything's so mixed up. I just need to—"

Adam grabbed my hands and slipped closer to my side, looking right into my eyes. Relief flooded me. *This* was the Adam I knew. The crease of his eyebrows, the tremble of his lips, the way he looked at me like he knew all of me—these things showed that he actually cared, that he hadn't forgotten what we meant to each other.

"Don't for one second doubt yourself, Maggie," he said, his words shaky. "Joey was *not* mad at you. This . . . thing, it was between us. And I have to figure it out before I can say anything, okay? You and Shan are the only ones who know about the argument, and I need to trust that you'll keep this quiet."

"I don't know," I said. "You're really scaring me, Adam."

I readjusted myself on the rock, pressed my feet into the prickly grass, and looked down at my toes. The paint was chipped, almost gone, but the color was the same. Totally Teal.

And that's all it took.

Whirl. Swirl. Twirl.

Back to the woods.

Adam's sea-glass eyes, his crinkled lips, his damp hair. Clinging. I was clinging. His hand, tight as a vine. The scramble down the trail. Tanna's wet braids. Trembling. And Shannon. Her eyes darting everywhere, crazy with pain.

"Oh, my God."

"What?"

"I remember. You. Finding me. My bare toes in the leaves. The climb down. Seeing Tanna. And Shannon."

Adam's hands squeezed mine. "It's not your first memory, is it?"

I shook my head. "I've had a few others."

"I knew it. That night at the Walthers' you were so off balance when you mentioned being at the top of the cliff, when you talked about me telling you not to look down for too long. I thought maybe it was because Joey's mom was asking so many questions. But I wondered if the memory was new." Adam let go of my hands and looked down to the rippling water. "And you haven't told anyone yet?"

"The memories, they're just pieces," I said, rubbing my palm across my forehead. "I need more time, to see how many I can get back. To put all the slices together again before I can talk about it."

"That's *exactly* how I feel, Mags." Adam sighed. "I need more time before I can talk about the stuff that was going down between me and Joey."

I breathed in the damp, muddy scent of the fishpond, wishing I could make sense of everything that had happened. "I was glad the memories were gone. At first. But now . . . I want to remember everything."

Adam stood up then. "Don't pressure yourself, Maggie. The memories'll come back when they're ready." He held a hand out between us.

"I hope so," I said, grabbing his hand and letting him pull me from the rock. I shoved my feet back into my shoes. "Can we make a deal?"

Adam held a hand over his eyes, blocking the sun. "What kind of deal?"

"We're gonna tell each other everything. *Everything.* When we're ready."

Adam closed his eyes and sucked in a deep breath.

"Please, Adam."

"Just give me a little time, okay? For now, we gotta go in there," Adam said, turning toward the back of the church. "You ready?"

I shook my head. "I don't think I could ever be ready for this."

"The viewing's over soon. I don't want to walk in late for the service."

I clutched Adam's hand and followed him across slick blades of grass, lit so brightly by the sunlight they almost glowed, and into the dark chamber of the hushed church.

My legs went numb as Adam led me down the center aisle, and I was glad he was there to lean on. I tried to block out the sea of heads, the sets of shoulders cloaked in black (frilly, sheer, lacy, cotton). Some people from school turned to stare as Adam and I made our way to the reserved seats in the front row, to our places with Shannon, Pete, and Tanna. Others did their best to give us the privacy we needed. I tried not to notice. Tried to ignore everything. Especially Joey.

As I dropped onto my cold, hard seat, I focused instead on Shannon. I stared intently at her jittery feet, her black ballet flats tap-tap-tapping each other in the quiet hush that had fallen over the room. I watched her long fingers, wrestling with two tattered tissues. And I listened to the stuttered sound of her breath as she struggled to keep her composure.

When the pastor stepped to the podium in a swooshing flutter and spoke with a reverent tone saved for especially devastating occasions, I closed my eyes and blocked out everything. Everything except my curiosity about Joey and Adam's argument, because that was the one thing that I *knew* I could figure out. And maybe, if I started with the things that I knew for certain, the rest would fall into place without me having to try so damn hard.

8
A Whole New Normal

"They're making me see a shrink," I said, stuffing a cracker into my mouth and crunching down. "Tomorrow."

"Really?" Shannon pulled the top off her strawberry yogurt and dropped it into her lunch bag. "That sucks."

"It's because of the memory loss." I sighed. "Among other things."

Tanna looked at me, her silver barrette blinking in the bright light of the early-June day. A June that Joey would never see. "Talking to someone could be really good for you, Maggie."

"I guess," I said. "It might help me remember."

"Mags, it just happened," Tanna said. "You need to give yourself a little time."

I leaned my head back against the trunk of the tulip tree that we had claimed as our lunch spot the first day of sophomore year. This was my favorite place on the campus of Blue Springs High School, and had been since I'd spent freshman year staring out the window of my geometry classroom watching the tree change through the seasons. Bright yellow and red leaves during the fall gave way to a slender, snow-covered frame through the winter. Then, in the spring, waxy tulip-shaped leaves filled out the branches just before these crazy bright yellow and orange flowers popped open to decorate my view, celebrating the end of geometry and the fast-approaching summer.

"Hey, Maggie," a voice called from behind us.

I turned to see Jimmy Dutton standing there, his hands stuffed in the front pockets of his droopy cargo shorts, a backpack slung over one shoulder. His hair was all messy, sticking up in places. He looked so much like the last time I'd seen him, when Joey had been alive and standing right by my side, that my chest started to ache.

"I didn't get the chance to talk to you last week at the, um, funeral," he said. "I just wanted to tell you how sorry I am about Joey."

I tried not to react to his name, but my breathing hitched a beat and caught in my throat. I forced myself to stare at the lingering petals that had fallen from the tulip tree, fluttering on the ground near my feet.

"Thanks, Jimmy," Shannon said.

"No problem," Jimmy said. "I keep thinking about the party. Seeing him for the last time, racing down that driveway. I can't believe he's—oh, God, I'm sorry. I sound like an ass-hole." Jimmy slapped a hand to his forehead and yanked his fingers through his hair. "Really, though, Maggie, you were out for a week, and exams are in a few days, so I just wanted to let you know that if you need my notes from English or wanna talk about the test, I've got everything you need."

I looked up, squinting at the bright blue backdrop behind him. "Thanks, Jimmy. I'll let you know."

He stood there for a minute, awkward, like there was something else he wanted to say. And then he turned and walked away.

"I feel like I'm under a microscope," I said. "You guys getting this, too?"

Tanna shrugged. "Not like you, with it being your first day back," she said. "I see the way everyone's watching you. Like you're going to shatter, or scream, or something else that'd be text-worthy."

Shannon grunted. "He was closest to you," she said. "I mean, everyone knew it. And you were the one with him when . . . well, when it happened."

I detected something strange in her voice. Something I couldn't quite put my finger on. For one horrible moment, I wondered if she blamed me. I wanted to ask, but I was afraid of her answer.

"People are just clueless," Tanna said. "They have no idea what to do."

Shannon tossed her empty yogurt container and plastic spoon into her lunch bag and pulled her knees to her chest.

Across the quad, Adam and Pete pushed their way through the back doors of the cafeteria. Adam looked at the ground, his body slumping, like he was caving in on himself. It was the first time I'd seen him since the funeral, since he'd chosen to ignore all of us when we'd hung out Saturday night. Pete had been worried when Adam didn't show—I could tell by the way he chewed on his lip—but he kept it to himself, trying to cheer us up by playing songs on his guitar and making us guess which memory the music had come from. Every single one he'd chosen had been a perfect Joey moment, and Pete had actually gotten us laughing.

Missing Adam that night, I had thought seeing him would make me feel better. But he'd walked the other way when I'd called out to him in the parking lot earlier in the morning, and in the classes we shared, he seemed to be avoiding me, his eyes focused downward at all times. Surprisingly, seeing him had only made me feel worse.

"How do you guys think Adam is doing?" I asked.

Shannon looked out over the quad, her eyes stopping on Adam and Pete. "Not good," she said.

I looked at her, at the slope of her freckled nose, how wild strands of her hair waved in the breeze, wondering exactly how much she knew about the fight between Joey and Adam. I felt floaty. In a very bad way. Like nothing around me actually existed. I pressed my hands into the ground, digging my fingers into the dirt.

"All of this avoidance, it's because of whatever happened the night of Dutton's party, right? There was obvious tension between Joey and Adam." I said. "What do you think was going on?"

Shannon tossed her hair from one side to the other, like she was trying to shake off the conversation. "Dunno," she said. "And I think we should leave it alone until Adam's ready to talk."

"But he's totally blowing us off," Tanna said. "Even Pete hasn't talked to Adam since the funeral. He told me this morning."

Shannon pointed. "They're talking now."

I looked up and saw Adam and Pete passing over the brick path that crisscrossed the quad. They stopped about a hundred feet from the tulip tree, fist bumped, and then Adam turned and started to walk toward the parking lot.

"Where's he going?" I asked.

"You haven't been here," Shannon said. "He hasn't exactly been eating with us."

"That's putting it mildly," Tanna said.

"Then, where's he been eating?"

"Adam's been ditching," Tanna said. "Like, every day."

"Well, I'm sure his parents—"

"They have no idea," Shannon said. "I talked to his mom yesterday when she called my mom about some fundraiser they're doing for the library, and she said something about how school seems to be helping Adam keep his mind off things. Whatever the hell that's supposed to mean."

I watched Adam's backpack disappear around the corner of the gym, wondering where he was going and what he would do when he got there.

"Did you say anything?" I asked.

"To his mom?" Shannon asked. "Um. No. We took that oath, like, a thousand years ago. We don't rat each other out."

"Unless," I said, "one of us is in trouble. And Adam is starting to show some signs of serious trouble, Shan."

"Why?" she asked. "Because he's skipping a few classes and not eating lunch with us? Because he needs a little space? Think about it, Maggie, he just watched his best friend die. You can't expect him to act normal. These days, we're dealing with a whole new normal."

"I don't know," I said, imagining Adam walking straight to the creek in our neighborhood and following the twisting trail of the stream until it swirled out into our Jumping Hole. All alone.

"You haven't exactly been normal yourself, there, Miss Memory Loss," Shannon said, scrunching up her nose. "Should we go talk to *your* parents?"

"That's not fair," I said. "I'm trying here. But Adam . . . it seems like he's just gone, somehow."

"I see what you're saying," Tanna said. "But I think we need to give him some space. Let's just get through the end of the week and see how he seems after summer break starts."

"You think?" I asked.

"I do," Tanna said. "We're all dealing with this differently. He deserves a mourning period, and we should offer him a little peace."

"She's totally right," Shannon said.

"Fine," I said. "If you guys think he's okay. But it won't be long before I insist on a full-scale intervention."

And I was serious. If Joey could die and Adam could slip away, what would stop the rest of my world from disintegrating into nothing?

I stared down at the lined notebook paper in front of me. At the thick black ink staining the page, the scientific terms and definitions I was trying to memorize all blurring together. I wished with everything in me that I could slide full speed down the neck of the *J* I'd drawn in the bottom corner of the page, fling myself off the hooked end, and flip into another existence.

But there was no other existence. My life consisted of quick glances, open arms, hushed whispers, pointing fingers, tear-soaked cheeks—all of which were about two seconds away from causing me to lose it.

I wanted out.

A free pass out of my body and mind.

During the last nine days, I'd been continuously hoping for some escape.

A way to release everything.

If only I'd known that the wish might backfire, bring me more pain, I might have taken it back. But I didn't know. Not as I sat there pressing the tip of my pen into the groove of the *J*. Not as the door behind me opened and another person stepped into the small conference room of the guidance office. Not as Nolan Holiday plopped his backpack next to me and sat on the rolly-wheeled chair to my left.

"Glad you're back," he said, running a hand through his longish brown hair. "This whole office aide gig has been lame without you." He ducked his head, meeting my eyes for a split second before deciding it would be better to stare at the floor.

"Can't say I've missed it," I said, looking through the large windowed wall as a skinny freshman boy juggling a load of books walked in from the hall and up to the secretary's desk.

"You missed a lot of drama," Nolan said, his eyes

sparkling with deviousness before turning dark. "Oh. I didn't mean . . . God, that was stupid."

"I coulda guessed that about the drama part."

"I was talking about our favorite budding romance. The one that was cut short." He grinned, slicing a finger across his throat. Then his eyes dimmed again. "Shit, man. Should I just shut my mouth?"

"Awkward is my new normal," I said, knowing how to put on a well-rehearsed, I'm-just-fine face. It was worth it just to avoid everyone's strings of questions (*How are you holding up? Are you taking care of yourself? Can I do anything?*) and the general awkwardness that Joey's death had left behind.

"That blows," he said. "The whole thing just bl—"

"It's okay," I said, leaning back in my swivel chair and facing Nolan Holiday head-on. "I know you're talking about Mr. and Mrs. Sophomore Suck Face, and I'd love a distraction, so please fill me in."

"Sweet. I've been dying to tell you." Nolan clapped his hands and rubbed them together, leaning forward. "Mrs. Suck Face's father came in, demanding to know how a picture of his daughter being, and I quote, *felt up* in the school hallway managed to be taken and posted on Facebook."

"No way," I said. "Did you see the picture?"

"Hell, no," Nolan rolled his eyes. "As if I have any interest in a flat-chested sophomore? But Mrs. Suck Face's father was quite entertaining as he met with the guidance counselors and Principal Edwards, demanding to know how such behavior could possibly occur in an educational environment."

"What'd they say to that?" I asked, grabbing my purse and riffling through the contents.

"The wall interfered." Nolan tipped his head toward the wall separating the small conference room, where we were, from the larger one. "All I heard after that first part was mumbling. Until the end, when Mrs. Suck Face's father stormed out, saying that the administration had better make it more of a priority to monitor the students in the building."

"Oh, God," I said, plucking a pack of gum from under my iPod. "That's pathetic. He'd rather blame someone else than face the problem that's right in front of him."

"Thought you'd enjoy a detailed description." Nolan smiled, his eyes catching mine as I unwrapped my piece of gum and popped it into my mouth.

"Thanks. Nice three-minute distraction." I smiled and held the pack of gum between us. "Want one?"

Nolan grabbed a piece, his fingers grazing mine and pulling back as though he'd been shocked, like he was afraid he could catch death from me. The thought of electricity running between us sent a shiver of something familiar through my body. I shook it off, though, forcing myself to stay in the moment.

"You okay, then?" Nolan asked as he slowly pulled the silver wrapper off his piece of gum.

"I'm not gonna freak out or anything," I said, hoping that would remain true. Somehow, over the past week, I had gone from being on the brink of freak-out ninety-nine percent of the time to about . . . seventy-five percent of the time. Until, of course, some random thing brought

Joey rushing back. At first, I never thought I'd get used to the idea of Joey's death, but it had settled over me like a fine mist. It had started to feel like reality instead of a bad dream. "It sucks. But I'm dealing."

Nolan looked up at me, his head still tilted down a bit, his brown eyes searching mine for any hint of truth or lie. "Yeah?"

I shrugged.

Nolan shoved his gum into his mouth and crushed the wrapper up into a tiny ball, staring down at one of the blue tile squares on the floor. "It's just weird," Nolan said. "The whole death thing. Everyone's talking about the last time they saw him or talked to him."

I scooted forward on the seat of my rolly chair, inching toward him, longing for one more slice of Joey's life to add to the patchwork of memories I had begun to assemble. Wishing I had access to my last seconds with him, hoping I would remember soon, that I would finally find the full truth and have my own story to tell in moments like these.

Nolan looked at me, his eyes watery and reddening. "Sorry. That's probably the last place you wanna go."

"No!" My voice bounced off the walls, too loud for the room. "I want to know as much as I can. Any new memory, even if it's not mine. . . . They all seem to help, you know?"

"Yeah?"

I nodded. "Will you tell me? Everything you remember from the last time you saw him?"

Nolan shook his head. "It's really nothing, though."

"Please," I said, something desperate flaring, and surging, and spreading through my body. "It's crazy, I know, but it helps keep him alive just a little longer when I hear other people's stories."

Nolan swung his head to the side and wiped his eyes.

"Did you see him the night of Dutton's party?" I asked, hope blossoming in my chest. Maybe Nolan was the key to finding out what Joey had been doing after he taken me, Shannon, and Pete home.

"No, I was out of town that weekend with my parents, picking my brother up from college. Heard the party was a blast, though." Nolan leaned back in his seat and propped his hands behind his head, elbows splayed outward. "Last time I saw Joey, actually talked to him, I mean, was at the Spring Carnival."

I shook my head, trying to jar the words loose before they took root. "Joey wasn't at the carnival."

Nolan's eyes creased. "Yeah. He was."

"You must have mistaken someone else for him," I said with a forced laugh, feeling a nervous tingle flash through my body. "He went to a Reds game with his dad that night. Killer tickets, or something like that."

"Oh." Nolan's entire face crinkled up and he looked away, dropping his hands into his lap. "Okay. I must've been wrong." He pulled himself up to the desk and grabbed his backpack, opening the front pouch and taking out a blue pen like he was ready to end the conversation and start his homework. As if Nolan *ever* did homework during our office aide period.

I reached for his hand, stopping him. "Well, maybe Joey came late." I glanced up at the ceiling, trying to look confused or thoughtful or something that would keep Nolan talking. "I was kinda drunk." I giggled, as if what I said had been funny.

Nolan squinted, looking unsure. "It *was* late."

"God," I said, smacking Nolan on the arm, needing that memory. "You're acting so weird. Just tell me already."

"Right. Okay." Nolan sat back in his chair, click-click-clicking the top of his blue pen. "I had to work that night, so I got to the carnival late. It was dark already, and there were about a zillion cars in the parking lot, all lit up from the flashing lights on the rides."

I flipped back to that night in an instant—it had been several weeks ago, one of the last days in April. Tanna, Shannon, and I had vowed to ride every ride before we left. Pete and Adam had laughed at us, saying we were acting like we were ten again. And then Shannon almost puked while we all were on one of those spinning things where the floor drops away from your feet. So we abandoned our plan, laughing as we passed a stick of pink cotton candy among us, leaving Pete and Adam behind.

"I had to park in the back of the lot, where it was super dark and shadowy," Nolan continued. "That's where I saw his truck."

I wanted to stop Nolan there. To tell him that all kinds of people drove black trucks and it would have been easy to mistake Joey's for someone else's. Especially in the dark. But I was afraid that if I spoke again, I'd ruin my chance to hear the story. A story I was certain was wrong. A story I wanted to deconstruct so I could prove that Joey was exactly where he had said he'd been. Because one thing I knew for certain was that Joey was *not* at that carnival.

"I didn't see him at first," Nolan said, "but when I walked by the truck, Joey shot his arm out of the driver's side window and grabbed my shoulder. Scared the living shit out of me."

"So, you actually *did* see him? *Talked* to him?" I sucked in a deep breath and held it. I couldn't keep breathing. Not with this in the air.

"Yeah . . . I mean, it was only for a few minutes. He gave me some shit about how I squealed like a little girl. I made fun of him for hiding in the shadows. Then I promised I'd get him back when he wasn't looking. That kind of thing. I told him he'd had a good game the night before. I remember that part. I also remember how, the whole time we were talking, he kept looking in his rearview and checking his phone. I just figured he was . . ."

"What?" I asked, holding a shaky hand in the air.

"I figured he was in trouble with you over something." Nolan shrugged. "I didn't want any drama, so I said *later* and walked away."

My heart was about to explode. Joey really was at the carnival? Why hadn't he told me?

"He was, wasn't he?" Nolan asked. "In the doghouse?"

"No." I shook my head. I felt as if it might swim away from my body.

"Oh, shit, I knew I shoulda kept my mouth shut."

"No. It's okay. I asked. I just wish I knew what had him so bothered, is all."

"Don't know." Nolan chewed his gum so hard it seemed like he wanted to pulverize it.

"Strange." I tugged at a strand of my hair and wrapped

it around my finger, pulling harder and harder until I felt pain. "That's all?" I asked. "You don't remember anything else?"

Nolan shook his head. "I'm sorry, Maggie. I never woulda—"

"Nolan, it's fine. Totally fine." I shrugged. "He must have been waiting to surprise me. Give me a ride or something. But Tanna took me home, and her car was, like, right up front. We got a great spot. So he wouldn't have seen me." I sounded pathetic, more pathetic than Mrs. Suck Face's father, the king of avoiding what's right before your eyes, and we both knew it. Whatever had brought Joey to the carnival that night had been something he'd intentionally kept to himself. Just like whatever he'd been doing after he dropped me off the night of Dutton's party.

"Right." Nolan slid his chair forward and tugged a notebook from his backpack, flipping it open without looking at me. He clicked his pen one last time. "Makes complete sense."

But it didn't.

It made no sense at all.

Not unless Joey was keeping major secrets.

As I sat there hearing echoes of the carnival music, feeling the breeze drift across the heat of my cheeks, tasting the sweet fire of the raspberry vodka we had poured into our sodas, I wondered. . . . What else had Joey been hiding from me?

And more importantly, why?

9

Forget You

"I can't believe you're making me do this." I tipped my head against the cool glass of the passenger-side window, closing my eyes against the bright sunlight that was trying to convince me it was a happy kind of day. "It's just weird."

"Maggie, the police said you have to be evaluated." My mother sighed.

"You're taking the easy way out, blaming them," I said, looking right at her.

"You want me to tell you that I think it's a good idea?" My mother slowed our black Hyundai Tucson to a stop at a red light in downtown Blue Springs. "You suffered a major trauma, Maggie. And you're dealing with memory loss. I think this is the best—"

"Really?" I asked. "Did you even look at those intake forms? The questions are for someone who's really messed up, Mom. Not me."

"No one's saying you're messed up, hon. Just that you need a little help with all that's happened."

"What I need," I said, "is *Joey*."

I swiveled my head so I wouldn't have to look at my mother. I couldn't get a handle on my emotions. Part of me felt relieved that I might be a few hours away from some answers. *If* this woman could help me access my memories, which was a big *if*. I'd been trying nonstop on my own when I was alone in my room, focusing on what I knew for certain. But I had yet to uncover anything new. The other part of me was just plain scared. What if talking about everything made it all feel worse? I wasn't sure I could handle worse. It might break me all the way.

"I know this is scary for you. I'm still asking you to give it a try."

"Asking?" I tilted my head toward the window again. "As if I have a choice?"

We spent the rest of the ride in silence, moving beyond the center of Blue Springs, with a Dairy Queen on one corner and a 7-Eleven on the other, through miles of corn and soybean fields.

The ride relaxed me, put me in a trancelike state. I focused on the things that didn't hurt. The trees, how they were so thick they looked stronger than I ever expected to feel. The wide fields, so green they almost shimmered. The deep blue sky, so vast and open, it felt like I could dive right through its surface and disappear.

After about thirty minutes, we hit the town just south of ours, Bradyville, which was smaller than where I had grown up. The first houses we encountered were older, and a few leaned, almost like they were drunk. Bradyville is a farm town, and as soon as we crossed over the county line, I lowered my window. I had always loved that Bradyville seemed to be drowning in the scent of hay, so I focused on the sweet, comfortable feeling it brought me. When we passed by a park, I stared at the kids hanging off the playground equipment, their laughter filling the air, chasing the silence out of our car.

I was okay for those few moments, while my mind drifted from one thing to the next, because none of it had to do with Joey. Or the cliff top.

But then I saw the high school. And I remembered my last trip here, less than two months ago, when I'd had to take the ACTs in a musty-smelling science room because I'd been sick the day they had them in town.

I'd stood against the wall next to the double doors of the high school's entrance, rain falling all around me, slamming into me with sweeping gusts of wind. Trying to avoid being soaked, I pressed my back against the scratchy red bricks but still ended up looking like a drowned and droopy version of myself. Which was the last thing I wanted, because Joey would pull up and see mascara running down my face, like I'd been standing there crying over him.

I was tempted to jump out into the rain, to look up at the sky and scream. But the sky hadn't deserved my rage. Neither did the little red Ford Taurus my grandmother had sold me for one hundred dollars, which was in the shop getting a new transmission.

My anger was all directed at Joey, who was late-squared picking me up.

Since my cell died during the first break in testing, I didn't have a way to check my messages. I used another girl's phone, calling Joey three times as the sky darkened overhead and rain began to fall. But the connection just rolled me over to his voice mail. When the girl's father came to pick her up, I was left completely alone.

I stood in the rain, shivering, feeling like a fool, wondering what to do.

I was seconds from walking two miles to the nearest convenience store to call my mom for a ride when Adam's light blue Oldsmobile pulled into the front lot of Bradyville High School. I was as surprised to see him as I was grateful that he had come. I hopped into the front seat, shaking from the cold and my anger at Joey. Adam threw a towel at me, and I wrapped it around my shoulders to warm up.

"Where is he?" I asked.

Adam just shook his head, his lips pinched tight. "Dunno."

"Whaddo you mean, you don't know?" My teeth chattered as I looked at Adam. "You're here instead of him, so I know you guys talked. Is he still fighting with his mom? Did she take his phone?"

Adam's body was tense, rigid. "Something like that."

"Well, I don't see why she wouldn't let him at least answer his phone to make sure I'd get home okay. I almost walked two miles in this shit to use a pay phone because my cell died and—"

111

"He's just a guy, you know?" Adam looked at me, his eyes sparking in the dim light.

"What's that supposed to mean?"

"You put him up on a pedestal, like he can do no wrong. Trust me," Adam said, "he can."

"I know he's not perfect."

"Coulda fooled me."

"This isn't his fault," I said. "His mom's a freak about his curfew. He was, like, three minutes late and she totally flipped her shit. Joey has never done anything like this before."

Adam grunted.

"What?" I asked. "What's that supposed to mean?"

"He's never done *anything* like this before? What about homecoming?"

I snorted, flinging my hand in the air, dismissing the long-ago memory, which I had shoved from my mind as soon as Joey had explained himself. "That wasn't his fault. His mother made him go to his grandparents' that night, and—"

"Right. I remember." Adam shook his head. "And Joey forgot his phone in the rush to leave, so he couldn't call you to explain anything."

"His grandfather had a *stroke*, Adam. I was probably the last thing on his mind." I slid lower in my seat. "Besides, he did call me."

"Yeah. At, like, eleven o'clock. When the dance was almost over and you were still sitting in your house waiting for him." Adam looked out the windshield, his eyes squinting as he tried to focus on the road through the thick wash of rain that the wipers couldn't keep up with.

"If I recall correctly, we had the best pizza of our lives that night." I poked Adam in the arm. He elbowed my hand away.

"It was okay."

"Okay?" I asked. "It was the best. Really."

"Just because it was hand delivered by the biggest stud in town."

I laughed, the sound rushing out of me.

Adam looked at me and grinned. "The studliest stud."

"M-hmm." I poked Adam again, glad that a smile had lit his face. "If you're such a stud, why'd you drop your date off before midnight, huh? Most studs would have been getting it on until dawn."

Adam shrugged. "I felt bad for you."

"Liar."

"I did." Adam looked at me, his eyes tight. "I felt awful when you called looking for him. You'd spent the whole night all dressed up alone in your basement, wondering where he was."

"Well, it was still nice of you." I twisted my wet hair behind me and tucked it into a bun so it would stop dripping down my back.

"Yeah. It was." Adam looked at me and rolled his eyes. "It was also nice of me to stop and get your favorite treat to make you feel better after waiting so long today. Three devil's food from Bozie's Donuts. I even grabbed you a hot chocolate. Thought you might be cold." Adam passed me a steamy cup of hot chocolate, and I sipped from the plastic lid. The foamy top was sugary sweet, and the drink was the perfect temperature after Adam's

113

long ride into Bradyville, warming me from the inside out.

"Well," I said, "if anyone's in the running for perfect, I'd say it's you."

Adam finally smiled. "You just remember that, girl. You hear?"

"Only if we can blast a song of my choice."

Adam threw his head back and groaned. "No. *Please*, no."

"I deserve it," I said. "I stood there for almost an hour not knowing what the hell was going on."

"Fine," Adam said, leaning toward the windshield as several gusts of wind rocked the car. "Blast your crappy music. Scream at the top of your lungs. See if I care."

"You rock, Adam." I leaned forward then, ruffling Adam's rain-stained hair. From the corner of my eye, I caught him watching as I hooked my iPod into his system and twisted the dial. I wondered what he was thinking. But just for a moment. Then the fearless sound of "Forget You" by Cee Lo Green surged through the car and carried me away.

"So, Maggie, today's session will be for us to get acquainted, and to set some goals for your treatment." Dr. Guest sat back in her swivel chair and tipped her head toward me, strands of auburn hair escaping her loose bun and falling to frame her face. Her legs were uncrossed, and her hands lay still on top of the open notebook on her lap.

I looked around the office, reading the framed degrees

that certified Dr. Patricia Guest as a licensed professional clinical counselor and a doctor of psychology.

"You're just about to finish up your junior year of high school, right?" Dr. Guest asked.

I nodded, sliding down the seat of the brown leather couch.

"And I hear that you have a very tight-knit group of friends." Dr. Guest smiled. My eyes flitted from hers to the tray of snacks on the coffee table between us. Did people really have the stomach to *eat* during these sessions? I couldn't believe that a handful of peanuts and M&M's made a person feel safe enough to open up.

"Let's start by going over some of the forms you completed for me." Dr. Guest lowered her voice. She suddenly sounded like a real person. "You mentioned that you don't really want to be here, Maggie. Can you tell me a little more about that?"

"Don't take it personally," I said as she stared at me, her eyes searching every flicker of movement that my body made. "I don't really want to be anywhere anymore."

"What about your friends? Does spending time with them give you any sense of security?"

I sighed. Tried not to think of Adam, all the voice messages and texts he had ignored over the last week. But he was there, mixed in with everything else, and the thought of his absence, once again, stirred a feeling of uncertainty in my chest.

"We're all just trying to deal," I said.

Dr. Guest pressed her lips together and gave me a slow

nod. "It can be very difficult, finding balance at a time like this."

I looked up at her, wondering how, after spending only five minutes with me, she'd hit on my biggest fear in life—never being able to balance everything out. Finding my lost memories and dealing with what had happened on the cliff. Living this new life without ever seeing or talking to Joey again. Blending the old version of Adam with this new, out-of-reach person he had suddenly become. None of it seemed possible. And that scared me more than anything ever had.

"You described your feelings, here, Maggie." Dr. Guest looked down at her notebook, shuffling through a few loose papers, and I caught a glimpse of my handwriting, the ink from the teal pen I'd used to scribble answers to all of those questions. "Shock is definitely a normal reaction to losing a person you love. And this fear you mention? Can you explain that for me?"

"Aren't you the one who's supposed to do the explaining?"

Dr. Guest smiled. "I'm here to guide you, Maggie. But I can't do that if we don't have a dialogue."

"Right," I said, taking in a deep breath. "So, the fear? It's just there"—I placed a hand on my chest and pressed it against my cotton shirt—"all the time."

"Fear about what, exactly?"

"Everything," I said. "But mostly just the realization that all it takes is one moment for your entire world to turn upside down. One wrong decision, and it's over."

"I understand, Maggie. This must be a terribly difficult

thing for you to process. The trauma of losing someone you love, being there to witness the event, it can—"

"But I don't remember anything," I said. "So it's not like I actually *witnessed* it."

Dr. Guest sat forward, her elbows propped on her knees, keeping the notebook in place. "Yes, Maggie, it is. You might be repressing the memory, but you were there. Everyone places you at the top of the cliff. You, yourself, even say that you remember climbing the trail with Joey."

I flinched at his name. I wanted to stand up and run. Forever.

"So, what? I have a classic case of memory repression?"

"That's what we're here to figure out." Dr. Guest smiled. "You're not alone, Maggie. I'm here to help you through this."

"What if I don't want your help?"

Dr. Guest shrugged. "The police requested that you be evaluated. It might take some time, but I'll determine your diagnosis, and we'll go from there. I'm here for the long haul if you need me."

"Diagnosis? Like I'm sick?"

"Why don't we stop trying to label everything and just talk?" Dr. Guest flipped through the forms again, my words swimming together to create a teal puddle in her lap. "You say here that your main goal is to remember what really happened on the cliff top. Is that still the case?"

I sucked in a deep breath and looked her right in her blue-gray eyes. I was shaking. My hands. My legs. I wanted to find my lost memories, but I didn't want to do it this way. I just wanted to be in my room, shoved deep in the cave of my closet.

"How do you . . . you know, do that with someone? Find memories that have slipped away?"

Dr. Guest leaned back in her chair, her hands falling over the paper that was dripping with my words. "There are several methods, and we can discuss them to see which you might be most comfortable with."

Sitting there, talking about my memories, wondering what we would do with them once they were found, I was suddenly hit with a question. One that had been bouncing around in my mind since I'd stood up from the table in the police station and walked away from the two detectives. And I had to know the answer.

"Do the cops think I'm faking or something?"

Dr. Guest's eyes pulled tight. But it was only for a second. And then she picked up her pen. "Why would you ask that?"

I shrugged. "They're calling this an official investigation. Questioning all of us. Searching through Joey's private stuff. And they sent me here to be evaluated. I just wondered, is all."

"Now is not the time to worry about any of that." Dr. Guest scratched something on the page of her notebook without looking down. "Today, let's just get comfortable with each other."

I sighed. Wove my fingers together and squeezed tight.

Dr. Guest straightened herself and looked me right in the eyes. "You said that you don't want to be anywhere anymore. Does that mean that you're thinking of hurting yourself?"

I squeezed my eyes shut. If only it were that easy. "No."

"Good. That's very good." I heard the pen scratching on the paper again and opened my eyes. "Why don't you tell me a little about Joey."

I smiled. I couldn't help it. But then the prickly feeling came back. The one that had been lurking beneath the surface of my skin since that day at the cliff. I closed my eyes for a beat, shoving that awful feeling away, and focused on Joey. My Joey.

"He was amazing," I said. "Beautiful. And a little crazy."

Dr. Guest grinned.

"He loved music, and his truck, and being outside. Oh, and baseball. But he could play any sport. He was a natural athlete. Actually, when I think about it, he was kind of a natural at everything. Life—it just seemed to come easy for Joey."

As soon the words were out, I wanted to capture them. Shove them back inside. Because thinking about his life brought me right back around to his death.

"What, Maggie? What about saying those things made you catch yourself?"

"I think about it all the time," I said, looking down at my hands again. "That day. Focusing on what I remember, trying to find the rest. But I don't get anything new."

"That's very brave of you." Dr. Guest sat back in her chair and nodded. "Many people in your situation would probably prefer to keep it all buried. But I believe that finding those memories and dealing with your emotions will help you move on more successfully. Facing what happened is the best way to keep this from weighing you down for the rest of your life."

I squeezed my hands tighter. Looking down, I saw that my fingers were white. "Even if I remember everything, it's going to weigh me down," I said. "I feel like it's pulling me under."

"I'm on your side, Maggie." Dr. Guest leaned forward again, wearing those pleading eyes. "I need you to trust me."

And that was all it took.

Flip. Dip. Trip.

I was back on the cliff top. Looking into Joey's eyes. There, right in front of me, I could see his freckled nose, the wisps of damp hair clinging to his forehead, the way his smile tilted to the left.

I wanted to reach out and grab him. But I blinked, and he was gone.

It was just Dr. Guest and me in the too-cool office with the whistling sound of the air-conditioning drowning out the heavy cadence of my breathing.

Dr. Guest stood and stepped around the table. She sat next to me slowly, as if I was a wild animal that she might scare off. "Maggie. Can you tell me what just happened?"

"I was back. At the cliff top."

"And how were you feeling?"

"Scared. Terrified."

"Of what?"

"Jumping. I'm afraid of heights. Like, pass-out afraid."

"Okay. This is good, Maggie. What did you see? Hear? Smell? Tell me everything."

"It was just a flash." I blinked and saw him again.

"Can you try to describe what you saw?"

"Joey." I could barely hear my own voice. Dr. Guest moved closer. She smelled like peaches. "Joey's face. He was smiling."

"Do you remember anything else? Even if it doesn't seem to fit, did anything else come with that vision of Joey?"

I shook my head. But I was lying. I heard him loud and clear. His voice washed through me like a warm and tingly wave.

You trust me? he'd asked.

I had.

Oh, I really always had.

10
All We Have in Common

"Have you heard about the cliff?" Shannon asked, rocking slowly back and forth on the recliner in her basement. "I saw on Facebook that a bunch of people went out there the other night, and—"

"I don't want to talk about the cliff," Adam said, leaning back on his bar stool, running his fingers along the stubble of his chin. I wondered when he'd shaved last. If he'd even bothered since the funeral, two weeks ago. The usual golden shimmers had turned a dark brown with the length. Somehow, in the last three weeks, he'd aged about ten years. I felt like I didn't even know him anymore.

Shannon slid her legs down the front of the chair and leaned forward, looking right at Adam. "I was just going to say that people have been taking flowers and notes and stuff there. I saw a picture."

"That's kinda creepy," Pete said.

"It's nice, though." I leaned back on the couch. "In a slightly creepy way."

Pete sat on the floor in front of me, crossing his legs and pulling his dreads back with an elastic band. He tucked his caramel-colored acoustic guitar against his body, strumming his fingers slowly across the strings, spilling a calming melody into the air around us. "It doesn't feel real yet. I half expect him to rush down the steps and laugh at us for being so freaked out."

Tanna looked up from the vodka and Hawaiian Punch drinks she was mixing at the bar. "It'd be nice if this was just one of his pranks."

"Can we *not* talk about Joey?" Adam asked. "For one freaking night?"

I stared at the looping strands of carpet, so soft on my bare feet that I felt like I could melt into the ground. Pressed myself farther into the back of the couch, gripping my hands in tight fists. I started counting: seconds without Joey, the ways Adam seemed to be changing, all the things Joey would never have the chance to do. I allowed the simple *one, two, three* to take over, to crowd out everything else.

"You okay, Adam?" Tanna asked as she rounded the corner of the bar holding two glasses filled with her special, pink-tinted drink. She crossed the room, handing one of the glasses to Shannon and the other to me, her hair spilling over her shoulder.

"I'd be better if we could just move on," Adam snapped.

"I don't get it," Pete said. "You just want to erase him? Like he never existed?"

Adam snorted. "Something like that."

"That's cold, man." Pete gripped the neck of his guitar,

his fingers tight across the strings. "We're talking about a guy who has been like a brother to you most of your life, you know?"

Adam looked at Pete, but didn't say one word.

"This is the kid who traded his favorite baseball card to get you a video game for your birthday in sixth grade," Pete said. "The same guy we've played basketball tourneys with every Friday during the summer since middle school. And let's not forget Independence Day."

"Aw, man," Adam ran a hand through his hair and squeezed his eyes shut, "why the hell are you bringing that shit up?"

"Because, for some reason, it's like you've forgotten who he is."

"What's so important about of the Fourth of July?" Shannon asked, looking from Pete to Adam. "Haven't we spent all of those together since, like, birth or something?"

Adam and Pete exchanged a glance, and I thought I saw the shadow of a smile creep across Adam's lips. Tanna slid a glass across the granite countertop into Adam's open hand, the pinkish liquid sloshing over the side, and then grabbed the remaining two. She sipped one as she took the other to Pete and sat cross-legged next to him on the floor.

"I'm talking about a different kind of Independence Day," Pete said. "It's been our secret since the year we found the Jumping Hole."

"Care to share?" Tanna asked, laughing. "I mean, you can't just tease us with something like that."

"You do the honors." Pete tipped his head toward Adam.

"It's not that big of a deal," Adam said with a shrug.

He'd seemed to soften some with the memories Pete had brought up, and I hoped that our plan was working.

"Must've been kind of a big deal," Tanna said. "I thought there were no secrets with us."

Adam sighed and looked up, focusing on each of us before he spoke. When his eyes met mine, I felt something crack open in my chest, and the full weight of everything we'd lost hit me again. It happened like that—a song or a scent, the sad look in someone's eyes—something simple and seemingly innocent brought the feelings rushing in, like that day at the cliff was happening all over again. Then the fear sliced through me, the terrible fear that nothing would ever be the same again. Not just with Joey, which had obviously changed forever, but with all of us.

I took a deep breath, focusing on Adam's lips, waiting for his words to wash away the sting of my fear.

"We found the Jumping Hole that summer between seventh and eighth grades," Adam said, his voice soft. "It was me, Pete, and Joey, remember? Being there, so far from everything, just gave us this sense of total freedom, so we decided to claim July thirteenth—the day of discovery—as *our* Independence Day."

"There's a tradition, too," Pete said with a smirk, "but that's top secret. We took an oath, swearing we'd never tell."

Adam shook his head. "I don't see why it matters now."

"Don't you get it?" Pete asked, leaning toward Adam. "It's up to us to keep him alive."

"I'm just not into it." Adam shook his head. "I don't think I can, bro."

"Why?" I asked, anger flaring through every inch of me. I'd felt like we were getting somewhere, and then Adam trampled all of my hope in the same moment that he trashed Joey's memory. "It's not like he ever did anything to you." My voice was cold, my words sharp.

"You're right, Maggie," Adam said. "He never did anything to me."

"So why are you so pissed at—"

"This," Adam said, hopping up from his bar stool and twirling a finger in the air, "was a bad idea. I'm gonna hit it." He turned then, starting for the steps toward the main floor.

"Wait," Tanna said, throwing a hand in the air. "Just sit, okay? We need to talk to you."

Adam looked around the room. I wondered if he knew what was coming. That we'd planned tonight just so we could ask him about why he was suddenly too busy to hang out with us. That we weren't going to let him go until he talked to us. That we were here trying to pull him back. And even though he'd pissed me off, even with all my fear that he'd push us even farther away, I still hoped he would actually let us in.

"You guys need to talk," Adam said, sitting down again, placing his hand on the bar. "Talk. But do it fast, because I'm not hanging around for long."

"Fine," Pete said. "We're worried. You seem so pissed off all the time. And you're avoiding us."

Adam took a swig from his glass. "I'm not avoiding you," he said with a shrug. "I'm just doing my own thing."

"It seems like a hell of a lot more than that," I said. "You never return my calls."

"Mine, either," Tanna said.

"We're a week into summer, and you haven't even stopped by to play basketball in my driveway," Pete said. "Doing stuff without him isn't wrong, it's a way to honor his memory."

Shannon tucked herself into a ball on the recliner in the corner near the fireplace, rocking slowly back and forth. She sipped the pink drink and rested it on her knee. "I practically had to threaten you to come over tonight."

"You, threaten me?" Adam took another gulp, leaving his glass almost empty. "That's funny, Shan."

Shannon looked up to the ceiling, scraping her nails down the legs of her blue striped pajama pants.

"Dude," Pete said, strumming a few chords on the guitar. "Not cool. She's trying to help."

"I don't know what the hell you guys want from me," Adam said, tossing his hands in the air.

"We want to know what's going on," Tanna said. "Why you're so angry. And why you're acting like you hardly know us."

"*We* are not *us* anymore," Adam said. "It's like all we have in common right now is the most fucked-up thing that's ever happened in any of our lives."

I couldn't handle it, couldn't keep quiet for one more second. Even though I didn't know the specifics, everyone needed to understand that Adam's issues were a lot more complicated than he was letting on.

"Tell them, Adam," I said.

"What?" he asked, his eyes snapping to me.

"Tell them. Or I will."

Adam took the final sip from his glass and plunked it down on the bar, shaking his head.

"Adam and Joey were fighting," I said. "The night of Dutton's party. And if he would just tell us about it, so we could all help him understand—"

"What will you help me understand?" Adam asked. "That Joey was all kinds of perfect and we should bow down to his memory? Well, Maggie, he wasn't perfect. Truth is, he wasn't even that—"

"Shut *up*, Adam!" Shannon jerked forward in her chair. "Stop trying to make it seem like Joey was the bad guy. I saw what happened at Dutton's. And Joey did, too."

"What are you talking about?" I asked, looking from Shannon to Adam and back again. "Since this whole phone call thing came up, you've sworn you didn't know why they were fighting."

"Please, Maggie. Like you don't know?" Shannon snorted and sat back in her chair, rocking back and forth with her movement.

"Wait," I said, "what am I missing? I have to be missing something because I feel like I just slipped into an alternate universe."

"I'm talking about *you two*," Shannon said, pointing to me and then Adam. "The way you were dancing that night. Joey might have been across the yard, but he saw you. And from my perspective, it sure as hell looked like something sketchy was going on."

"You can't be serious," I said. "You were dancing *with* us."

"No," Shannon said. "I definitely wasn't."

"Oh, my God," I said. "I can't believe this is—"

"Shannon, don't do this." Adam's voice ripped through the air.

I shot up from the couch, staring Shannon right in the eyes, hating her.

"Are you seriously accusing me and Adam of—"

"Look," Shannon said, "I'm just calling it like I saw it. You two seemed pretty close that night. And since Adam isn't sharing specifics with us, I'm simply taking a wild guess."

"Well, you guessed wrong," I said. "Way wrong."

"Whatever you say." Shannon's lips turned up in a little smile that I wanted to scrape right off her face. In that moment, I might even have scraped her out of my life for good. But angry as I was, it was still Shannon. And with Joey gone and Adam in some kind of crisis, we had to stick together. So I just turned away from her and pressed my lips together.

"This has been real," Adam said. "But I'm over it."

"Adam, you still haven't—"

"You expect me to spill my guts after that?" he asked, tossing a hand toward Shannon. "Don't count on it."

He turned and raced up the steps, taking them two at a time, disappearing before I could even begin to grasp what had just happened.

I stood there staring after him, tugging at the sleeves of my sweatshirt, Joey's favorite baseball hoodie. It was light gray and had deep front pockets that I used to love digging my hands into when Joey was wrapped in its warmth. I'd done it often: waiting in line for the haunted hayride last Halloween, hanging out and sipping hot chocolate after ice-skating in the center of town last Christmas, and walking through the hall between classes when I tucked a note in the soft darkness as we kissed a quick good-bye.

And now, standing in Shannon's basement, with the last trace of Adam's energy quickly fading from the space around us, with his anger, Shannon's accusations, and Joey's secrets spiraling all around us, I shoved my hands deep into those pockets, feeling like I'd just said good-bye in a whole new way. To Joey, the only boy I had ever loved; to Adam, the guy who'd always been there, but suddenly wasn't; and to a lifetime of friendship that I never thought would fade.

11

Secrets of My Own

Like Joey, I had secrets of my own. Plans that I'd never shared with him. Questions I'd never admit to. Things that gave me the rush of excitement and daring he probably felt on a daily basis, Joey being Joey and all. Most of them were good secrets. Secrets that, if he'd learned of them, would make Joey break out that lopsided grin that had been spinning my world on its axis for most of my life. And the rest—those secrets Joey might not like so much. But those didn't matter. Those were mine alone. Dreamy, private thoughts that would never exist outside the safety of my mind.

"Seriously?" Tanna's eyes widened and a smile spread across her face. She leaned forward, the thick braid that she'd twisted her hair into slapping against my arm as she pulled me into a hug. "You're gonna be all grown up, Mags."

Shannon made a sound that was between a snort and a snicker and took a swig from the can of Milwaukee's Best in her hand. "You're sure you're ready?"

I looked over my shoulder, catching a quick glimpse of Joey as he bounded through a crowd of people who were all cheering as Jimmy Dutton kicked his feet up in the air for a keg stand. Joey took the back patio steps of the Duttons' enormous house two at a time, his hand breezing across the wooden railing. Light spilled out of every window causing Joey to practically glow as he opened the screen door and stepped into the kitchen. I could still feel the kiss he'd planted on my forehead when he ran by, telling me he had to pee and then he'd be back with drinks.

"It's the little things," I said, staring through the bay window of the dining room so I could watch Joey stand in line for the bathroom, bouncing from one foot to the other, his baggy tan shorts swaying around his muscular legs. "All the little things make me sure it's right."

"For some reason, I'm guessing it's *not* very little." Shannon giggled and pressed her fingers to her lips.

"Shannon!" Tanna smacked her on the arm. "Maggie is confiding a secret of supreme importance. Have some respect."

Shannon raised her hand to her forehead, pulling her face into a tight mask, and saluted Tanna. "Yes, sir."

"She might be drunk, but she asked a good question." Tanna plopped down in the green lawn chair at the base of a large oak tree in Jimmy's backyard, ignoring the chaos of the party surrounding us. Three topsy-turvy seniors stumbled past in a blur of long arms and legs, rushing through the flickering shadows of the Duttons' backyard toward the sound of Pete's guitar, accompanied by a banjo and harmonica as he and two friends played some fast-paced bluegrass song near the fire pit. "You're sure you're ready?"

I listened to all the laughter. There was so much of it. Everywhere. I could almost see the looping strands of sound coloring the air around me.

"It's a good party," I said.

"I can't believe it's Memorial Day weekend. We're almost *seniors*." Shannon propped herself against the oak tree and looked up into the leafy branches.

"Mags," Tanna said, her eyebrows arched. "You're ignoring me."

"No." I shook my head, looking back through the bay window to find Joey standing right in front of the closed bathroom door. He was knocking on the dark wood and, from his profile, I could tell he was laughing. I knew the sound of his laughter so well, I felt like I could hear it pulsing through the walls of the house, carried by the bright light streaming through the windows. "I'm thinking."

"If you have to think about it," Shannon looked right at me, "you're *not* ready."

"That's not true." I could hear the defensive tone in my voice and wondered what color it would be if it floated into the air, mixing in with all the happiness surrounding us. I pushed the thought away and looked at Joey again, finding the curve of his neck, where I planned to kiss him first when he returned with a fresh beer in his hand. "Thinking about it means I'm being responsible. And that's what makes me ready."

"Nope." Shannon shook her head. "What makes you ready is feeling that you might *explode* if you wait one more second to be with him."

"There is that." Tanna sighed and straightened the striped skirt she was wearing, tugging it up a tad to show off more of her tanned legs. "But thinking about it is good, too. Preparing. Knowing."

I laughed then, out loud, the sound rippling into the night and riding the air to far-off places. "I *totally* know."

Tanna looked at me and gave me the loudest *squee*. "This is huge," she said. "We'll have to go shopping. You need something *sexy* to wear."

My stomach did a little twist. "Sexy?"

Shannon pushed off the tree and walked over as I sank into the chair next to Tanna. "You gotta show Joey that you feel him," Shannon said as she leaned against the back of my chair.

When I looked for him again, Joey was gone. In his place were four girls, giggling and red faced. I imagined that he'd said something to make them all flutter before he closed himself into the bathroom.

"Oh, he'll know I feel him," I said. "I'm just not a Victoria's Secret kind of girl."

Shannon kneeled down in front of me, draping her arm across my legs. "If you're planning to lose your virginity to the guy you've been dating for almost two years, you need something sexy. He deserves it for being so patient, right?" Shannon's eyes flickered between me and the bay window. I turned to find Joey exiting the bathroom, tugging up the zipper on his shorts and high-fiving the senior captain of the baseball team as he passed on his way to some deeper part of the house.

Joey's eyes sizzled with life. I could practically feel their heat.

Tanna kicked me, the heel of her sandal biting into my shin.

"Ouch!" I leaned over and tugged on her braid. "What'd you do that for?"

"We're discussing the details of your first time, and you can't focus long enough to commit to a shopping trip?"

"You said his parents are going out of town?" Shannon lifted her eyebrows and took another swig from her drink.

"His parents'll be gone for an entire week, just after school lets out. I've been planning it since I heard." I giggled at the way my insides went all shiver-shaky at the thought of Joey's naked body on top of mine. "You wanna go shopping next week, fine. Maybe you're right."

"Ladies." The deep voice came from behind us, and we all turned to face him.

"Adam, where have you been?" Tanna asked. "This party is in, like, full swing. You're gonna have to do at least five keg stands to catch up."

Adam chuckled, pushing his bangs away from his eyes with the palm of one hand. "Shan didn't tell you she saw me earlier?"

"No," Shannon said, something strange crossing her face. "I forgot."

"Well, I've been in the crowd"—Adam nodded toward the ever-growing circle of people clamoring around the fire pit, most of them bouncing to the beat of the bluegrass—

"listening to Pete jam with G and Rusty. They're rockin' it out."

I closed my eyes, tipped my head back on the chair, and focused on the sounds drifting across the backyard. I pictured bright reds and oranges spiraling through the air, a spiking strand of yellow thrown in here and there, all tumbling from the instruments, twisting around the people, and bleeding out to color the night sky. It was one of those moments where everything in my life felt right. I had these awesome friends. And the best boyfriend, ever, to whom I was about to give myself completely. Summer was about to begin, and when it ended I'd run smack into my senior year of high school, which I'd only been thinking of reaching since sixth grade. I felt in sync with everything around me. Even the drunk people stumbling around the yard. But especially Joey.

I plucked my head from the back of the chair and sat up, my brain swimming in all the beer I'd downed. "Where's Joey?"

"Pee break, remember?" Shannon threw a thumb toward the kitchen door.

I shook my head. "I saw him come out of the bathroom. He should be back with the beer now." Not that I cared about the beer. I wanted him to swing me out of my seat and dance me, barefoot, across the cool carpet of grass. The music, it was infectious, streaming into my body, and I needed to get up and move to the bucking banjo and taunting harmonica, to the threads of guitar pulling it all together. It was the song, a twangy version of Snoop Dogg's "Gin and Juice," that had done it to me.

136

"I want to dance," I said with a giggle. I knew I was drunk, but it was a nice heavy feeling, like a warm blanket, and not out of control.

Tanna looked at me with a smile. "Dance?" she asked, placing her beer in the grass. "You want to dance?"

I laughed, nodded my heavy head. And then my hand was in Tanna's. She pulled me from the chair and swung me around, my hair lifting off my shoulders and dancing right along with me. Shannon joined in, and the three of us sang along to the lyrics like it was our song and no one was there to watch us.

Soon, Adam's feet were in the mix, his brown sandals kicking up into the air with my bare feet, Tanna's heels, and Shannon's flip-flops. We twisted around one another, shouting the words, linking arms, trading places as our voices and happiness flew out into the night.

It was at the very end, when the song slowed down, that I found myself in Adam's arms. His grasp was tight around my waist, keeping me steady as I belted the lyrics out to the dark night that lay beyond the reach of the fire's light. I leaned into him, closing my eyes, focusing on nothing but the sounds Pete and the guys were flinging into the air. I breathed Adam in, the scent of him damp and hot, a spice so different from my Joey. But so familiar-good.

As the last notes sounded, I looked up at Adam, tugging a strand of hair from his eyes. He tilted his head down, gave me a wink. And right there, in the Duttons' backyard, with people dancing all around us, drunk on music and alcohol and summer, I started to wonder. . . . If I kissed him, eyes closed tight, where would I feel his hands first?

137

If his lips met mine, would it be soft and sweet? Or rushed and insistent?

Then Shan laughed and Tanna bumped into me, pushing me right up against Adam's chest. The way his eyes flashed when I pressed my hands against him made me wonder if all the stuff rushing around my head had invaded him, too. But then I let it go, tossed out all those questions until they disappeared. Because I had Joey, who was all kinds of amazing.

"I think you need to sit down," Adam whispered into the loose strands of hair tickling my face.

He squeezed me close as he guided me back toward the chairs. I just breathed. Focused on the in and out. If I focused on all the rest, guilt would come flooding in. And I hadn't done anything wrong.

"That was . . . ," I started, but couldn't find the words to balance the thoughts that were still echoing through my mind.

"Nice," Adam said.

"Yeah," I whispered as Adam dropped me into the chair. "Very."

Adam took a step back, moving me from a pool of darkness to light in the space of one single breath. And that's when I saw him, staring out at me from the top step of the Duttons' back deck. His face was in shadow, but I could tell from the stiff slant of his shoulders that something was off.

I waved him over. But he just stood there watching. I wondered how long he'd been there. If he was upset that I'd been dancing with Adam. But Joey wasn't like that. Never had been.

Then I wondered if my thoughts had been so loud that maybe he'd heard them. If he knew I'd pictured Adam kissing me, and me kissing Adam right back. I wanted to explain. To tell him that it was a simple moment of drunken curiosity. I wanted to assure Joey that I would never, ever do anything to answer the questions that had been spinning around in my mind. But that would have been crazy, spilling all that out into the space between us. So my only choice was to act normal.

"Joey," I yelled. "C'mere."

That's what got him moving. The sound of my voice. He jumped the five steps, pummeling the grass with his feet, and bounded across the yard.

"Here you go." He handed me a beer and then passed one to Tanna and Shannon, too. "Didn't know you were here, man," Joey said to Adam.

"Got here a while ago." Adam's voice was tight.

"Mmm." Joey took a swig from his beer. "It's a wild one."

I looked up at both of them. They were standing next to each other, but they were stiff. Awkward. I felt like something was going on, and I hoped it didn't have anything to do with Joey knowing me so well he could read my thoughts. Then another song started, painting the irritation that drifted between them deep shades of dusty pink, indigo, and green, whisking it away after just a few notes.

Joey began to tap his hand on his knee. And then, without warning, his eyes flashed mischievously, and he started to speak. As always, he surprised me.

139

"I found something in there." He threw a hand toward the house. "Anyone up for a little excitement?"

"Way to be mysterious." Shannon hopped up from her spot on the ground, her wavy brown hair flying around her shoulders. "I'm totally in."

Adam shook his head, looking from Joey to Shannon. "You two," he said. His lips parted as if he were about to say more, but then he pressed them together, trapping the words.

"Leave it alone," Joey said, his eyes tight with irritation. "You don't wanna come along, fine by me. But don't spoil our fun, dude."

Adam grunted as Joey and Shannon turned and started toward the house. I squealed and jumped up, tugging Tanna with me. "Wonder if it's some secret passageway." I envisioned pressing Joey up against a curved wall, bound to him by total and complete darkness, and showing him with one single kiss how very much he meant to me.

"C'mon, Adam," Tanna called over her shoulder. "You need a beer, anyway."

I looked back and caught Adam as he took a few slow steps after us. "Come on!" I shouted, tossing my head toward the house, throwing myself off balance, thinking it was a good thing that Tanna was there to keep me upright.

12

Shaky Fingertips

"You *do* know it's summer, right?" Tanna asked from the other end of the line.

I pressed the phone against my cheek and slid off my bed, moving across the room to the mirror above my dresser. "I'm so pale, you can almost see through me."

"Exactly my point. And that, my friend, calls for a pool day."

"Tanna, I'm not sure." Guilt flared through my stomach. I felt like I shouldn't allow myself to go on doing all the stuff Joey couldn't. Like I'd be betraying him if I went to Gertie's Dairy Farm for ice cream or sat around laughing with our friends. But then Dr. Guest's voice trailed through my mind, a direct quote from our last session, asking me to list the worst things that could happen if I decided to go on living my life. And the worst thing I could come up with was the guilt, which Joey would have hated.

"A day in the sun will do you more good than you can imagine," she said. "Trust me."

"I don't know," I said, thinking of the other reason I didn't want to do much of anything anymore. "Is Shannon going?"

"Yes. But don't let that—"

"I don't think I'm ready to see her after the other night."

"It's been four days, Mags. If you let this drag out for too long, it'll get to be like Adam. A total disconnect."

"I'm not so sure I care," I said. "She accused me of cheating, Tanna."

"It was a heated moment. She wasn't thinking."

"Still, she threw it out there."

"We all know Shan can be a bitch sometimes. And considering everything that's happened with Joey, maybe we should cut her a break."

"Yeah. But what she said was just stupid," I said.

"Right. But Joey drunk equals Joey crazy. Who the hell knows what went down between him and Adam the night of Dutton's party? Or what Shannon overheard from that phone call after Joey dropped you off? Bottom line is she's one of your best friends. You don't want to lose her, too, so we just need to move on. To take a day to focus on the basics: bikinis, sun, and swimming."

I groaned and looked down at my feet.

"I'll need a few to get ready," I said, pulling the drawer on the right side of my dresser open.

"Well, make it snappy," Tanna said. "I'll be there in fifteen."

"I'm painting my toenails, at the very least."

"I promise this will make you feel better."

"I hope so. See you in a few."

I ended the call and placed my phone on the dresser, digging through my stash of nail polish, mentally cataloging everything I'd need for a day in the sun: sunscreen, magazines, iPod—

And that's when I saw it.

When my hand danced closer to the back of the drawer, aiming for a bottle of Perfectly Pink. There, tucked between the Totally Teal and Raspberry Sorbet was my rainbow-colored flower necklace. I was confused at first, and then I remembered. Stupid, stupid me. The Spring Carnival. Pete throwing colored balls through the open mouth of a cardboard clown, tossing his arms up in the air once, twice, three times. He'd won *three* prizes. One for me, one for Tanna, and one for Shannon. And the prizes he'd chosen had been identical.

I sat there, running the slippery beads through the fingers of my left hand, thinking that I'd been wrong. I wondered what it meant, that I was sitting there holding my necklace when Tanna's or Shannon's had been wrapped around the handle of Joey's closet door. But none of my conclusions made any sense.

And then I remembered Tanna pulling her hair off her neck, twisting it into a bun for one of the wild spinning rides, the elastic thread of her necklace snapping. Then there were the flashing lights of the carnival's exit, and the trash can we'd passed on our way out, Tanna's hand flinging her broken flowers in the trash as we traipsed through the gates and into the parking lot on our way home. Tanna's necklace, it was in some landfill next to a dirty diaper or a soggy box of Wheat Thins. And mine was in my hands.

The necklace in Joey's room, it had belonged to Shannon.

As I laced the beaded flowers through my fingers, I saw her. Eyes wide. A smile splitting across her face.

"I'm going in," Shannon had said, her sandals clicking on the blacktop of the parking lot as the carnival lights tripped across her face, reflecting in her eyes. She stood there, twisting the flower necklace around her thumb. "That Toby Miller is *hot-hot-hot*."

"You sure?" Tanna had asked. "Maybe wait until you're a little more . . ."

"Sober?" I'd asked with a laugh.

Shannon had burped then. Pressed a finger against her lips. Shook her head. "No way, guys. He'll take me home if he thinks I've been left behind."

Then she'd taken off, a shaky half skip, half run. When she was a few cars away, Shannon turned, her yellow skirt fanning out around her legs, motioning for us to step back. "Duck," she'd whisper-shouted. "Don't let him see you!"

Tanna and I watched from the shadows as Shannon tapped Toby on a broad shoulder, as he turned, as they spoke. He smiled, laughed, and ran a hand through his hair (choice *I-want-you* body language, according to Shannon). When he turned and started toward the shadows of the back lot, Shannon threw us a high thumbs-up.

Tanna tossed her head back and laughed in that wide-open way I loved so much.

"She gets anything she wants, doesn't she?" Tanna had asked as she slid into the driver's side of her blue Honda.

"It is amazing." I'd turned to watch Shannon disappear

between two dark minivans. To where I now knew Joey had been sitting, waiting for something. Something that, for some reason, had nothing to do with me.

"You're still pissed, aren't you?" Shannon leaned forward in the green lawn chair situated between Tanna's and mine and reached into her beach bag for a bottle of sunscreen.

I didn't say anything. Instead, I focused on three middle schoolers with deep tans as they flip-flopped past our chairs, laughing and juggling hot dogs, Slushies, and Twizzlers. My eyes followed them as they made their way to their towels, which were laid out on the large stretch of lawn in the back of Blue Springs Swim and Tennis Club. I found myself wishing I could jump out of my own life and into the simple happiness that seemed to enfold them.

"You *were* pretty harsh the other night," Tanna said, readjusting the straps of her bikini top.

"Yeah, whatever." Shannon rubbed white lotion into her shoulders and upper arms in quick little circles. "I'd had a little too much to drink; I started before you guys even got there. And Adam, he was pissing me off, acting like Joey means nothing to him."

I wanted to ask her if she really thought Adam felt that way. But there were more urgent questions. Like, what was her necklace doing in Joey's bedroom? And what else did she know that I didn't? But I wasn't sure where to start. Or where it might end. So I decided to wait until I figured a few things out before I dove into the questions that were making me feel nauseous.

I bit my lip, grabbing a magazine from the foot of Shannon's lawn chair, wishing I'd trusted my first instinct and avoided this pool day altogether.

"So, Shan," Tanna said. "Isn't there something you wanted to say to Maggie?"

"Right," Shannon said, throwing the sunscreen into her bag as she leaned against the chair's back, propping one knee up in the air with the casual-sexy vibe that she always tried to emit. "I'm sorry if what I said upset you, Maggie. I know we're all just trying to deal, and calling you out wasn't fair."

"It wasn't fair to me or Adam," I said, flipping to the middle of the magazine, zoning on an ad for hairspray where a girl with spiky hair walked into a nightclub. "I just hope you didn't push him even further away."

Shannon propped her sunglasses on her nose and tipped her face up to the sky. I could tell by the way her foot was shaking that she was agitated, close to leaping off her chair, even, but was trying to restrain herself.

"He'll come around," Shannon said. "We just need to give him a little more time."

I looked down at the magazine again, trying to escape through the doors of the nightclub with that spiky-haired girl. But before I could even read the stupid slogan, I was jolted as the five lifeguards blew their whistles simultaneously, ending the rest period. Peals of laughter rang through the humid air as kids dove into the water from all sides of the large pool. Three guys with long hair hopped into the crystalline water a few feet from our chairs, splashing us. I threw the splattered magazine back onto Shannon's chair. It was pointless, anyway, trying to distract myself.

"I'm burning up," Tanna said, standing and tossing a mess of damp hair over her shoulder. "I gotta jump in."

I looked up then, shielded my eyes from the sun that was positioned almost perfectly over Tanna's head.

"Anyone wanna join?" she asked.

Shannon grabbed the iPod sitting on her flowered towel, twirling the wires from the earphones around one finger. "Not yet," Shannon said. "I wanna listen to some tunes first."

"I'm game." I was glad to have an excuse to get away from Shannon and hoped the water might wash away all the uncertainty that had flooded me since finding my necklace.

I'd just swung my feet over the side of the lawn chair and was about to stand up when Toby walked by. I had about a millisecond to react, or I would have lost my chance altogether. It was his shoulders, broad and bare, tanned from his many days stationed at his lifeguard post, the same shoulders that I'd seen in the parking lot as we left the Spring Carnival. Those shoulders kicked my mouth into action. I wasn't sure exactly what I was after, or if I would find it, but if I didn't ask a few questions, I knew I'd never get rid of the uneasy feeling that had settled in my chest.

"Hey, Toby," I said, standing quickly, sure to speak over the steady roll of splashing and laughing coming from kids in the pool.

He stopped, turning only partially, the whistle hanging from a red string around his neck swaying back and forth across his six-pack abs. "Oh. Hey, guys." He gave us a half wave.

"How's your summer?" I asked, willing him to step a little closer.

Those shoulders swiveled all the way toward us, and I knew I had him. "Okay, I guess." His voice was tight. A little unsure. He was confused about why I'd chosen to talk to him as though we were old friends when we'd only ever spoken once or twice before.

"You working a lot?" I asked, tipping my head toward the nearest lifeguard chair.

Toby shrugged. "Just about every day. But it doesn't feel like work."

"Shan," I said, looking down to see that her hands were frozen in the air, her skinny little iPod clutched in one, the earphone wires dangling from the fingers of the other. Her eyes were wide. Her mouth hanging open. And that made me feel good. "This job would be perfect for you. You'd get paid for working on your tan." I giggled then. All of them looked at me like I was crazy.

"But I'd have to wear a one-piece," Shannon said, her voice quiet. "I don't do one-pieces."

Toby laughed. So I did, too.

"Hey, I wanted to thank you," I said, an idea forming as the words tripped off my tongue.

"Me?" Toby pointed a finger at his chest.

I nodded. "I know it was almost two months ago, but Tanna and I feel awful about leaving Shannon behind at the Spring Carnival. Total miscommunication. It was awesome of you to take her home."

Toby's eyes creased, and he looked from me to Shannon and back. "I don't have any idea—"

"Maybe Maggie's right," Shannon said, interrupting him, hopping up and grabbing his glistening forearm. "Is there an application or something? In the office? I mean, getting paid to sit in the sun sounds pretty nice. And my mom's been all over my ass to get a summer job."

"I think the schedule's full," Toby said. "But you can fill out an application, anyway. If you really want to."

Shannon turned and yanked the sundress off the back of her lawn chair, tossed it over her head, and grabbed Toby's arm again. "Let's do it," she said with a smile.

Toby started to turn away, but he stopped. Faced me once again. "Hey, Maggie. I'm really sorry about Joey. He was cool. A little insane, but cool."

I nodded. Smiled. But it was forced, so I had to look down.

Shannon tugged at his arm. "To the office?" she asked, urgency springing from each word.

"I gotta stop by the locker room. I'll meet you in a minute," Toby said. "Nice to see you guys." Toby nodded his head toward Tanna and me, and the two turned and started toward the clubhouse office.

"What's up with her?" Tanna asked, moving to stand next to me.

I watched the way Shannon's tiny little butt swayed from side to side, the wave of her sundress swooshing around her thighs. Her hand dropped from Toby's arm, and she moved away from him. Not much. But the distance was telling. I wondered if she'd ever had a thing for Toby Miller.

"What do you mean?" I asked.

"This thing with Toby. She's throwing herself at him. Totally against her rules."

"Maybe she's in love," I said. "Love makes you break all the rules, doesn't it?" My chest exploded, hot and heavy. The thought nearly knocked me down. But then I pushed it away. Because whatever had been going on between Shannon and Joey, it *couldn't* be that.

Tanna twirled her hair up on top of her head, tucking it into a makeshift bun. "I guess with Shannon, there really are no rules, huh?"

I shrugged. "Guess not."

"You coming in?" Tanna stepped toward the edge of the pool, the water sparkling, throwing diamonds of light across her tanned stomach.

"In a minute," I said, leaning down to reach into Shannon's bag. "I gotta call my mom to tell her I'm here. She wants me to check in every five minutes these days."

Tanna gave me a pouty look. Then, with creased eyes, looked at the phone my fingers were clutching. Shannon's phone.

"Mine's almost dead," I said, tipping my head toward my purse. "Go on without me. I'll be there in a minute."

"I'm heading over to the deep end," Tanna said. "Those college guys are here. I want to position myself for when they start to practice their diving."

I laughed. "Being fully submerged in water does nothing to flatter your figure."

Tanna tipped her head to the side. "Maybe not. But if I get a cramp and need help, they'll get a great view when they pull me out of the water."

"Tanna, you're very creative," I said as she hopped into the water with a little splash and a giant squeal.

"It feels awesome," she said, flipping to her back and swimming away.

I looked to the office and could see through the large opening at the window counter that Shannon was twirling her hair around one finger as she talked to several guys. I had a few minutes at least. Even if she wasn't interested in them, she was interested in them being interested in her.

As I watched her, my mind flipped through several incidents I'd forgotten. Little things that seemed like nothing. Until now. The barrette in Joey's car that she said she'd forgotten when he took her home after a football game. His shirt on the carpet in her bedroom, which he'd supposedly loaned her after she spilled pizza down hers at lunch one day.

I sat on my towel, turning my attention to that phone. Scrolling through her messages, my fingers and breathing and heart got all tripped up. I was scared of what I'd find. But I needed answers, and the only people who had them were either not talking, or acting like they didn't know anything.

I couldn't risk looking for too much. I was dying to. But there wasn't enough time. So I searched for the date. Friday, April 28. The night of the Spring Carnival.

I had to figure it out. If he was with her. To know for sure what I only suspected.

But as I searched the history of messages between Shannon and Joey, I found a string of texts from another, more recent night.

The night of Jimmy Dutton's party.

An entire conversation.

Right at my shaky fingertips.

12:53 a.m.: *Shan, we nd 2 tlk.*

12:53 a.m.: *What did A say 2 u?*

12:53 a.m.: *Ur nt gng 2 b happy.*

12:54 a.m.: *He's nt making threats, is he?*

12:54 a.m.: *Something like that.*

12:54 a.m.: *U dropped P off?*

12:55 a.m.: *Yup. I'm abt 2 leave.*

12:55 a.m.: *Get over here.*

12:56 a.m.: *B there in 10. Meet me outside.*

13

Hiding Out

"So this is where you've been hiding out," I said, stepping from between two trees and into the moonlight. The creek was directly in front of me, bubbling its way through the back edge of the park that bordered our neighborhood. Before the guys found the Jumping Hole, this clearing had been one of our favorite hangouts. Since Adam had started avoiding us, I'd imagined him here several times, wondering if he might be sitting with nothing but the rustling trees as his companions. But I hadn't been ready to investigate.

I stood there, still, trying not to think about where all this water had come from; that this creek was fed by the flow that came from the gorge—from our Jumping Hole—where Joey had spent his last moments alive.

Adam looked over his shoulder, as if he'd been expecting me.

"This is *one* of my hideouts," he said from his seat on a large rock at the edge of the water. I remembered a younger version of him, sitting in that exact place, his shoes tossed to the side, his bare feet plunged into the flow of the creek.

"I've texted you, like, a zillion times since yesterday." I'd been hoping I could find him alone so we could talk, just the two of us, to see if maybe I might be the one thing to bring him back.

"Been ignoring my phone," Adam said. "It's easier that way."

"Not for us." I stuffed my hands into the front pockets of my capris.

Adam patted the rock beneath him and scooted sideways to make room for me. I walked over and curled my legs underneath my body, bumping his shoulder as I sat.

"You okay?" he asked.

I took in a deep breath and shook my head slowly, side to side, tasting the moist scent of the earth, swallowing the ball of fear that had risen in my throat.

"Me, neither." The golden hues of Adam's blond hair practically shone in the night. Alcohol rode the wave of his words, a thick, syrupy scent that made my head swirl.

"You have something to drink?" I asked.

"M-hmm." Adam held a bottle in the air. The moonlight flickered through the leaves above us, playing with the curves of the glass, splashing light in all directions.

My fingers wrapped around the neck of the bottle, pulled it toward my lips. I only intended to have a sip. To simply feel the stinging fire racing down my throat. But I kept going. After several gulps, Adam pulled the bottle from my mouth, yanked it from my clasped fingers.

"That's enough," he said.

I swiped my hand across my chin, flinging droplets of the liquid into the night. "Since when do you have a vote?"

Adam grunted. "I'm still your friend, Mags."

"Coulda fooled me." I swung toward him, my hair falling over my shoulder.

"Then why'd you call me?" Adam's voice was tired. He seemed totally drained of life.

"I need your help."

Adam turned to face me, raising both eyebrows.

"I figured out who Joey was with the night of Dutton's party." I swiped some hair from my eyes, blinking away the frustration that had settled into every molecule of my body.

Adam straightened his leg and dropped his foot over the side of the rock, swinging it slowly back and forth, just above the surface of the water. He didn't look at me. And he didn't say a thing.

"It was *Shannon*. They were all worried about some kind of threat you'd thrown down. And then there's something strange about the night of the carnival. Remember how Joey supposedly got home really late from the Reds game? Well, that's *not* how it happened. My mind is racing to all these terrible places, but I don't want to go to any of them—I just can't—not until I know something for sure. So I'm asking you, Adam. What the hell was going on?"

Adam stared at the rippling surface of the water, the way the moonlight danced across the silver channels, as if I wasn't even there.

I grabbed his arm, pulling him toward me. "You *have* to tell me."

"I'm sorry, Mags." Adam shook his head.

"Adam, *please*."

Adam shifted his weight, twisting on the rock so he could face me. He hesitated for a moment, his eyes focused on mine. "Where did you hear all this?" he asked. "What happened?"

And then, though he remained perfectly silent, I heard his voice continue, a distant echo in my head. *What happened before the screaming?*

I pulled back, sucking in a shaky breath.

Adam recoiled like I'd shocked him. "Maggie, I'm sorry. I didn't—"

"Screaming?" I clasped my hands together. Tight. "There was screaming?"

Adam leaned toward me again, holding my hands in his. Somehow, the touch warmed my entire shaking body.

"Why are you asking that?" Adam's lips were tight and his eyes looked frantic. Wild.

I kicked my legs out, clawing my feet at the rock, trying to gain my footing.

Adam put a hand on my knee, and I saw a flash of blood. Remembered not knowing if it had come from him or from me.

"There was blood on your arm," I said. "It was *Joey's*?"

"Just relax for a minute, okay?" Adam pressed the bottle into my hand.

I took another long swig. This time Adam didn't pull it away. When I stopped, the spicy liquid dribbled down my chin, but I didn't care. "You asked me what happened before the screaming. At the cliff. Right?"

Adam took a deep breath. "Yes," he said. "I did."

"What else?" I asked. "What else happened? Because I can't remember now. Not anything."

"You didn't remember then, either." Adam stared at me, his eyes turning a silvery green in the moonlight. He looked so much like his old self that I almost believed everything since Memorial Day weekend had been a bad dream, and that, even if it wasn't, Adam would suddenly snap back to normal and be the friend I'd always known.

"Adam, you have to help me. I feel like I'm losing my mind here. I mean, everything from the cliff top is gone. And then you, you're gone, too—"

"Maggie, I'm not gone."

"It sure feels like it. You're one of my best friends, Adam. And it's like you've died, too. And then I find out some shady shit was going down between you and Joey. And somehow Shannon's tied into it. I'm just walking around bumping into random things and hoping I find some answers." But at the same time I'm afraid. What if those answers just confirm my worst fears? What if the things I can't even say out loud are true?

"You can handle this. The memories, they seem to be coming back in pieces," Adam said. "That's good, right? You've remembered a lot in the few times we've hung out."

"I've only remembered *one* thing without you, Adam. One. And it was a snapshot, not an actual memory, okay? You'd know that if you'd taken the time to be more available."

"Available?" Adam's voice changed then. It went from soft to charged with just one word. "To what? Help lead you through your feelings? News flash, Maggie, I lost Joey, too. And I'm dealing with my own feelings. Huge, suck-ass waves of feelings that are about to take me under. So, I'm sorry, but I can't carry you to the other side of this. I have to carry myself. And if that means there's a little distance, then you either deal with it or you don't. I can only take on what I can handle right now."

"I don't expect you to carry me, Adam. But I expect some honesty. I mean, this is *us* we're talking about."

Adam laughed. Stood from the rock and looked down at me. "Jesus, Maggie, do you ever stop?"

I wanted to kick his legs from under him so he would fall back down and have to face me. "Tell me what you know, Adam."

"You're asking the wrong person, Mags."

"What the hell is that supposed to mean? Why do you always talk in code now? Nothing you say makes one bit of—"

"I don't know how I can make it any clearer for you. There's nothing more I can say." He looked at me, his eyes filling with an emotion I couldn't read. "I'm sorry, Maggie. I really am."

And then Adam turned and stepped off the rock, moved through the trees and into the darkest part of the shadows until he disappeared. It was in that moment that I finally understood I'd lost him all the way. It hurt more than I'd expected it to, the pain crashing down on my chest until I felt like I could hardly breathe.

14

His Too Blue Eyes

"I found a package on the front porch for you," my mom said as I came down the steps the next morning. She was standing at the island, the newspaper spread in front of her as she munched on a piece of peanut butter toast.

"From who?" I asked, not really caring. With Joey gone and Adam so totally disconnected, nothing seemed to matter anymore.

My mother smiled, holding a small rectangular box in the air. It was wrapped in brown paper, with my name written on the front. No address or shipping labels. Just my name, which was spelled in block letters with a dark blue Sharpie.

"It's very mysterious," my mom said, sliding the package across the counter to me. "I think you have an admirer."

"Mom, please."

"I'm not saying that you have to jump into a new relationship right away," my mother said. "But you can't close yourself off forever. It's not healthy."

"Why don't you leave the therapy to Dr. Guest?" I said. "She's a trained professional."

"Well, it's something you may want to discuss with her. There will naturally be some guilt. But it's something you need to—"

"Mom, really," I said, walking behind her and tugging on the belt of her robe, "leave it alone."

My mother sighed, then turned to face me, holding her coffee mug with both hands. "I'm heading upstairs to get ready for work."

"Have a good day," I said as my mother made her way through the kitchen and to the staircase.

"Maggie," my mother said, stopping, her robe swaying around her legs. "I meant what I said. I know you and Dr. Guest have been focusing on your memories because recovering them is so important to you, and I know that a month is too soon to expect you to move on, but everything that comes next is just as important as everything that's already happened. Okay?"

"Right."

"Don't do that," she said, shaking her head. "Say what I want to hear so I'll—"

"Mom. I get it. Okay?"

She sighed. "I made you some pancakes and bacon. They're in the microwave if you want to zap them for a warm-up."

I thumbed the buttons on the microwave and grabbed the bottle of maple syrup from the counter, turning to look down at that package. Part of me wanted to rip it open. But another part of me wanted to throw it in the trash. In my life, surprises had lost their appeal.

But as I poured the syrup on my pancakes, the package sat there calling to me, and I had to know what was inside.

So as soon as I finished breakfast, I grabbed a pair of scissors and went back up to the privacy of my room, wishing the little brown-wrapped gift had the power to flip everything back to normal.

When I pulled the paper away, I was confused. Someone had left me a photo album, the front cover dotted with hand-drawn hearts. My first thought was that it was from Joey. That was the stutter my brain still suffered from, a misfire that made me instinctively believe that he was still alive. But even if he were still here, he'd never been the type to doodle pink hearts.

I reached out, expecting the book to send shock waves of emotion up my arm—love, loss, hope, regret.

Something inside me pulled tight with unease, but I told myself that was stupid. I had to convince myself that none of my fears were justified. That there was a perfectly good explanation for all the things Joey had kept from me. And that this photo album was probably someone's way to honor the relationship I'd had with him, cataloging our time together with photos I'd somehow never seen.

I held my breath, hoping with everything in me that someone from the yearbook staff or the school newspaper had searched through old files for pictures that had once been unimportant. I visualized a shot of Joey and me walking through the locker-lined hall, clasped hands swinging between our bodies. But that vision was quickly erased.

As I flipped open the front cover of that album, I saw the worst thing ever.

A picture.

Of Joey.

And Shannon.

Kissing.

Shannon had taken the picture. I could tell by the way her outstretched arm reached toward me that she'd been holding the camera, turned it toward them, and pressed the button the instant Joey's lips had touched hers. How she'd gotten the picture so perfectly centered, I'd never know.

But she had.

And there they were.

Sitting in Shannon's basement. On her couch. *Exactly* where I had been sitting just a week ago, when we confronted Adam about blowing us off.

Shannon was laughing, her eyes squeezed tight.

Joey, too, his parted lips pressed against hers.

I slammed the album shut. Pressed my palm into all those hearts. Willing it away, away, away. But it didn't disappear like I needed it to. Instead, the album seemed to grow heavier, holding me down.

It flooded me in an instant. Understanding that all of Joey's secrets revolved around Shannon. That everything

I'd feared most since finding that stupid necklace in my drawer was actually true.

His secrets. They weren't just his. Those secrets belonged to both of them.

Together.

I wanted to know how big it was. How long it had been going on.

But the only way to find out was to face everything in that album.

I was nauseous from just one picture. I didn't want to go on.

But I had to. There was no other choice.

"You have to face this, Maggie," I told myself. "Just do it. Fast."

And so I did.

I flipped through the pages, finding more of the same. Pictures of Joey and Shannon together in the woods surrounded by falling red, orange, and yellow leaves; eating ice cream while wearing wool caps and gloves; sitting lazily on a swing in the park in T-shirts and jeans. They were laughing, or kissing, or touching in almost all of them—through the seasons of at least one full year.

The others, the ones where it was obvious there was some special meaning even though I couldn't see either of them, those were creative, just like Shannon. A shot of their bare feet in the grass, her toenails painted a bright pink, his underneath, perfectly trimmed. One of a sunset melting into a bank of snow-covered trees. A picture of pebbles along the bank of a creek, gathered together to spell out their names.

Joey & Shannon.

So together.

And so very alone.

The last page was different. A folded piece of paper, creased and worn.

Joey's name written on the front flap in Shannon's loopy handwriting. In her favorite purple pen.

I yanked the note free, practically ripping it in my need to understand.

Maybe I had something wrong. Maybe this was old, whatever had been going on. I needed to believe it had all happened before Joey and I ever began.

As I started to read, I held onto that hope.

And quickly felt it all fade away on the tide of a new loss that somehow outweighed the darkness of Joey's death.

> *Joey,*
>
> *I know what you're thinking. What you've been thinking since this all started last fall. That this is bad. All kinds of bad. But it's not, Joey. Nothing that feels this good can possibly be bad. It might hurt some people, Maggie most of all, but we have to figure this out. And we have to get it out in the open before the damage can't be undone.*
>
> *School will be ending soon. Summer starting. And that gives everyone three months to deal. To understand. And to let go.*
>
> *They will. You'll see. They have to.*
>
> *I love you. And you say you love me. So this should be simple. I'll do it any way you want. So*

take the next few weeks to do what you need to do.
And then the summer will be ours.
   I'll be waiting.
   Always.
   Shannon

My hands were shaking so badly that I couldn't refold the note. So I balled it up tight and shoved it back under the thin plastic sleeve, flipped the album closed, and threw it on the floor. I scrambled to my feet, clawing my hands through my hair and wanting to scream so loud that everything around me would shatter to pieces. I was pissed. So very pissed I could practically see waves rippling from my body and out into the room.

But then I saw his face. His too blue eyes. And his smile. Staring right up at me from the frame on my nightstand. It was my favorite picture of us together, because we looked so at ease. Tanna had taken the shot after school one day just a few months ago, when we'd all gone to Getrie's Dairy Farm for ice cream. I was sitting on Joey's lap, one leg kicked up, with my head tipped back mid-laugh. Joey's arms were wrapped around me, his hands clasped around my waist. The hands that had touched Shannon. I didn't understand how the Joey in my picture could have been the same Joey that was tucked away in her photo album.

I slipped down onto my bed, curling up on the quilt my mother had mended with thread that didn't quite match the rest, feeling the pain well up fresh. Joey's death somehow hurt more, swelling inside me until I felt like I might burst.

165

15

The Countdown

They had always been so alike. Crazy and senseless, rushing into things without thinking. Plotting pranks together. Daring to dive down the most curvy sledding hill in town while I stood at the top trying to convince myself I'd be fine if I followed after.

She'd always looked at every boy but Joey.

And me, I was the opposite.

Cautious. Reserved. And Joey had always been my only interest.

When I thought about it, all of it, the years we'd spent growing up together, it made sense, Joey and Shannon together. More sense than Joey picking me.

And that thought nearly killed me.

But what sliced into me even more were all the things I should have picked up on. All the rushed glances I'd missed. All the spontaneous things they'd done together that essentially eliminated me from the picture.

How totally stupid I had been.

"Lookie there, lookie there," Joey said, running a hand along his chin as he stood in the middle of the Duttons' oversize, three-car garage. A few feet in front of him was a shiny black and green motorcycle, with paint that literally sparkled in the overhead fluorescent lighting.

"Joey," I said. "Please tell me you're not thinking what I think you're thinking."

Joey looked at me. His eyes sparking with the not-so-quiet kind of mischief he'd always been known for. "I promise I'll be good."

Tanna laughed out loud, the sound echoing off the white walls of the garage, the super-shined surface of the Duttons' black Jaguar, the riding mower, and the totally organized work space stuffed with every kind of tool imaginable.

"Good?" Shannon asked, poking Joey in the arm, and the back, and the gut like an annoying little sister. "I wasn't aware you knew the definition of that word."

Joey whipped around, grabbing Shannon's hand and twisting it behind her back. "What did you say?" He was smiling, and so was she, but Shannon was wriggling to pull away from his grasp.

"Let her go," Tanna said, jumping onto Joey's back, "or you'll be sorry."

"I can take you both." Joey's voice strained as he struggled to upend Tanna while keeping his grip on Shannon's arm.

And then I saw it, the one thing that would stop him

like nothing else. Tanna had a finger in her mouth and was juicing it up with fervor.

"Ears," I warned, "watch your ears."

But it was too late, Tanna had already plugged Joey's right ear with her slimy finger. Joey shuddered and yelped, releasing Shannon and flinging Tanna off his back as he jumped away.

"You are so disgusting," Joey said as he wiped Tanna's spit from the side of his face and the inside of his ear.

Tanna and Shannon fell into each other in a heap of giggles, giving each other a smacking high five in celebration of their victory.

"You," Shannon said, "are a bully."

Joey propped his hands on his hips and shrugged. Then he turned to look at the motorcycle again. I could practically see the thoughts flying from his perfectly beautiful head: *I want to ride, I need to ride, I will ride. . . .*

"Joey," I cautioned. "You said you'd be good."

Joey nodded. "And I will."

I sighed. "Thank God. I thought you were about to steal this thing."

Joey shook his head, his deep brown hair falling down into his face. "Nope." He turned and walked toward the door that led to the Duttons' mudroom. I stepped quickly behind him, my bare feet padding along the cool gray paint that covered the garage floor. Adam was right behind me. I could tell because he felt like a heavy load pressing against my back. Whatever had him so ticked was going to be problematic with the three-day break ahead. Memorial Day weekend was full of tradition, and if the guys weren't speaking, the gorge the next day would be awful and stressful, the partying would feel disjointed, and the overall mood would—

"Wait," I said, scrunching my eyes as Joey stopped instead of placing his hand on the doorknob and making his way back into the house. I could feel Adam's tension rise a notch or two behind me. "What are you doing?"

"I said I'd be good." Joey grinned, his lips tilting to the side a little in that sexy way that always made me feel light-headed. He stared into my eyes, the blue of his own practically glowing with the excitement of a promised rush. "And I swear I will. It's just . . . I can't not." With that, Joey turned and jabbed the little glowing button next to the door, and the steady hum of the garage door invaded all the spaces around us, vibrating everything, including my beer-soaked brain.

I shook my head. "It's not a good idea," I said.

"Yeah, Joey." Tanna stepped around me then, tugging at the braid that had come loose during her wild ride on Joey's back. "You've been drinking."

"But"—Joey crossed a finger over his chest, one way, and then the other—"I haven't had any of those Jell-O shots yet. And I haven't smoked a thing tonight."

"A crotch rocket, Joey?" Adam asked, the irritation in his voice bordering on outright anger.

I looked at the bike, my eyes skimming the words scrolled on its side—*Kawasaki, Racing Team, Ninja, ZX6*—which were a little fuzzy and out of focus. The full light of the garage made me realize I'd had more to drink than I thought.

"You've ridden a dirt bike at your uncle's, like, a coupla times," Tanna said. "You ready for this?" She pointed her finger at the motorcycle.

When I stared at the thing too hard, it began to look like a large grasshopper. A very fast grasshopper that I didn't want Joey riding. But I knew what would happen if we pushed him, especially me, so I kept my mouth shut.

"I rode my uncle's Harley last month," Joey said, pulling his shoulders back. "That thing was a beast. I can handle this baby. She'll be smooth. Like buttah." Joey ran a hand across the green bump that sloped toward the black leather seat.

"Don't worry, guys," Adam said. "He'll never get it started."

Joey smirked.

I could have smacked Adam for challenging him. One thing about Joey, he *never* backed down from a challenge.

"Now we're screwed," Shannon said, sitting on the workbench and looking down at the smattering of stickers that covered the seat: John Deere, Carhartt, Harley Davidson.

"Oh," Joey laughed. "You guys were already screwed." Joey turned on his heels and walked to a metal box on the wall, flipped open the little door, and revealed a plethora of keys hanging off tiny hooks.

"Oh, shit." Tanna pulled her fingers through the waves her braid had created, shaking her head.

"Joey," I began, trying to think of the right thing to say to talk him out of it.

"Don't bother, Mag-Pie. I'm going."

"I hate it when you call me that," I said.

"I know. This might be easier if you're pissed."

"No. Not so much. You can't just go around stealing people's—"

"What the fuck's going on here?" A red-faced and breathless Jimmy Dutton skidded to a stop on the blacktop driveway in the opening of the garage. "You guys shouldn't be in here."

Joey smiled then, a real beamer, and nodded his head toward the motorcycle. He ran a hand through his hair and whistled. "She's a beaut."

"Yeah. And she's off-limits," Jimmy said, his voice shaking. I wondered if he knew he'd just thrown a double on top of Adam's challenge.

I sighed, resigning myself to the simple fact that before the night was over, Joey would find a way to ride that motorcycle.

"Is she yours?" Joey asked, his voice as sweet and sticky as honey. Poor Jimmy didn't have a chance.

Jimmy shook his head. "My brother's. The brother that talked my parents into leaving me here instead of forcing me to go to the lake for the weekend. The brother who got us the keg. And the fireworks. The brother who would skewer me alive if he knew I'd let someone take his bike out for a joyride."

"Dude," Joey said with a chuckle. "I totally respect all that. And your brother's a cool guy. Graduated a few years ago, right? I remember the game where he dislocated his shoulder trying to keep the ball in bounds. He saved the team that night. We made it to the state tournament because of him."

Jimmy's face loosened a bit, his eyes leaving Joey for the first time as he glanced at the bike. "My brother saved every dime for a coupla years to buy this thing, man. If someone breathes on it wrong, he knows."

"I'll be careful," Joey said. "I know how to ride. Have been for years."

Lie. Total lie. He'd ridden that Harley three times. On the dirt road at his uncle's farm so the bike would land on softer ground in case Joey keeled over.

Adam shifted his weight from one foot to the other behind me. Tanna looked at me and raised her eyebrows as she twisted her hair back into its braid. Shannon smacked her flip-flop against the bottom of her foot over, and over, and over.

"Dude, I dunno. I swore I'd keep everything locked up. Especially my brother's shit."

"He'll never know," Joey said. "I swear he'll never know a thing."

Just then a screeching sound tore through the night. Jimmy turned to look over his shoulder as someone flew through the front door and started puking in the bushes that lined the walkway. "Oh, man," he said, rubbing the top of his head. "Look, whatever, okay? Just so you know, if you get caught, I'll tell the cops, my brother, and God himself that you stole the thing. If you go down, you're not taking me with you."

I almost reminded Jimmy that he would probably be going down no matter what. The party was supposed to be low-key but had started to rage as people poured down the long driveway in a steady stream, holding six-packs and coolers, lit cigarettes and joints, shouting to one another and pumping fists in the air at the luck of having such a secluded place to hang for the night. No way Jimmy would be able to clean this up before his parents returned. An entire month wouldn't be enough time.

"You rock, man," Joey said, smiling. "I'll be careful. Don't worry."

Jimmy shook his head and turned quickly, jogging to the puker. When he reached her, he tugged on her shoulders, pulled her up, and half-walked, half-dragged her farther from the house.

"Told ya." Joey turned toward us, a smirk planted on his face. "I'm gonna ride." He threw a key high up in the air, a key I couldn't recall him plucking from the metal box. I watched it loop and spiral, the overhead light glinting off its shiny surface. As Joey caught the key in one hand, I stood there wondering if it had been cupped in the darkness of his palm since he'd come out back to gather us for his mysterious adventure. An adventure that really had nothing to do with us.

Joey spun to face me, his eyes glinting with energy. "You comin' with?"

I looked at the motorcycle. Then back at him. "I dunno," I said, my legs feeling wobbly with the thought of trying to hold on. Wobbly good because my entire body would be wrapped tightly against Joey's, a prelude to the surprise I'd planned for the week his parents would be out of town. Wobbly bad because the thought of the bike's motion made me feel a little sick. "I'm kinda drunk."

Tanna giggled. "You," she said, "are a lot drunk. And I forbid you to risk your life on that death machine."

"Oh," Joey said, slapping a hand to his chest. "The confidence you have in me is overwhelming."

"Ask me if I care." Tanna stuck her tongue out at Joey.

"So I can assume that *you're* not interested in a ride?" he asked her.

"No freaking way."

Joey looked at Adam, then. They both smiled, and a fresh glimmer of their friendship ignited into the cool night air. "Dude," Adam said, "don't even ask."

Joey shrugged. "Your loss, bro."

Shannon stopped flipping and flopping her sandal and looked at the bike.

"You wanna?" Joey's voice cracked a little and he cleared his throat.

She shrugged. "I guess."

"You guess?" Joey threw his head back and groaned. "That is not the kind of enthusiasm I was looking for, Shan."

Shannon giggled. "I've never ridden a motorcycle before."

"Never?" Joey asked. "That's a tragedy. Stand up. Hop on."

Shannon jumped up from the workbench and fluttered her long arms in the air, clapping her hands and giggling.

Joey straddled the bike's seat and started the motor with a quick and easy turn of that little key. The sound was louder than I'd expected, flooding the large garage, vibrating my insides with an irritating tickle.

When Joey tipped his head at Shannon, she flung a long, tanned leg over the back of the leather seat, bouncing up and down as she slid onto its center and sidled up to Joey's back. I was jealous. The feeling ripped through me. I wanted to be the one behind him, and I almost told them to forget it, that I was going instead. But Tanna was right. I'd had way too much to drink, and it wouldn't be safe for Joey or me if I rode with him.

"All you gotta do is hang on," Joey yelled back at Shannon as he tugged her arms around his waist. "And don't lean too far when we turn."

"Wait," I said stepping toward them, "aren't you guys gonna wear helmets?"

Joey shook his head. "We're not going far."

Shannon whisper-shouted something into Joey's ear. He grinned and looked at me, Tanna, and Adam.

"Shan wants a countdown," he said, blowing a strand of brown hair from his eyes.

I turned and grabbed Tanna's hand, Adam's, too, and squeezed.

"Three," we shouted in unison. "Two! One!"

We threw our hands into the air, shouting, Tanna and I kicking our feet out in a little dance, and waited for them to take off.

Joey winked at me, smiled, and picked his feet off the ground, easing the shiny green bike out of the garage. A crowd had gathered, openmouthed and gawking, and they watched with drinks raised, cheering, as Joey and Shannon peeled down the long strip of dark drive that led to the country roads twisting through the edge of town.

175

16

A Slice of Something Beautiful

"Do you think you can ever really know a person?" I asked, shaking a handful of M&M's in my hand as I settled in for my fourth appointment with Dr. Guest.

"Are you referring to Joey?" Dr. Guest looked at me, raising her eyebrows.

"It's just a question," I lied, popping the M&M's into my mouth.

I hadn't told her about the cheating yet. I hadn't told anyone. I was afraid of saying the words, as though once they were out there, it would make the whole thing all the way true. I'd spent the four days since finding that album struggling with the idea that the real Joey was nothing like the Joey I thought I knew, trying to avoid facing the fact that the Joey I loved had never existed.

Dr. Guest flipped to a fresh page in her notepad, held it in the air, and turned it to face me. She started drawing squares on the paper. Little ones. Big ones. I listened to the scratch of her pen, wondering what insight she was about to share, enjoying the sweetness of the chocolate melting on my tongue.

When she'd filled about three quarters of the paper with different-size squares, all linked together, she looked at me. "You've talked about that patchwork quilt your grandmother made, how you ripped it the day Joey died."

"I stole it from the living room," I said. "It's on my bed now."

"Your question made me think of how a person is just like a quilt."

I watched in silence as Dr. Guest filled in the rest of the empty space with small, medium, and large squares. Then she swiveled in her chair, her knees bumping the table between us, and presented her patchwork piece of paper.

"I don't get it," I said.

"Think about your grandma's quilt. The whole thing, it's a work of art, a slice of something beautiful."

I looked at the paper, all the squares, imagining the blanket that I'd spread across my bed a few weeks ago. "Yeah."

"Like Joey. He was a slice of something beautiful."

I swallowed. Hard. Trying to keep the tears down. Because no matter how much he'd hurt me with all the shit he'd left behind, that was so true.

"A work of art," I said.

"But if you look closely at that quilt your grandmother made, I bet there are pieces that you don't really care for. Small patches of fabric that you can handle when you look at the whole, but that you would never choose for yourself if you were making your own quilt."

I thought of the scratchy gray wool that had once

been a part of my great-grandmother's Sunday dress.

"Just like Joey. If you look closely enough, there are pieces of him that you probably don't care for. Pieces of him that, since his death, you're seeing for the first time. Pieces that might be ripped or torn. Imperfections. Ugliness. And that's okay."

"But what if, when I look really close up, I realize those small pieces that I don't like, all the imperfections, are bigger than the whole of him that I thought I loved?"

"Then you do what you would do if he were still alive. You let go." Dr. Guest looked at me with very sad eyes. "And you move on."

"But I don't want to. Joey, he is"—I sucked in a deep breath—"*was* everything to me."

"That's how people get into trouble, Maggie." Dr. Guest pressed her lips together. Then she let out a big sigh. "I sense that something has changed since we last spoke. You want to fill me in?"

I thought about letting the words spill into the room. But I couldn't say them yet, so I just shook my head.

"It's important for you to allow yourself to feel whatever you need to feel right now. Get angry. Cry. Scream if you have to. Move through this in the way that suits you best, and don't worry about Joey. He'll come back to you, even if it feels like you don't know him right now. You know, deep down, that you knew him very well."

But I didn't. I didn't know that at all. And that scared me more than anything.

"So, how do I remember?" I asked. "All the stuff that I left at the cliff. How do I go back and find it?"

"You reclaimed a memory the first time you were here. Have you remembered anything more?"

"I try every day," I said. "I sit by myself and concentrate on being there, on seeing and feeling and hearing everything that happened."

"And?"

I threw my hands in the air. "Nothing! All I get is the stuff I never lost, or the few flashes that have already come back."

Dr. Guest looked to the floor, shook her foot a few times, and then looked right at me. "I want you to think back to the times the memories have returned. Tell me about what you were doing, where you were. We need to find your trigger."

I almost laughed. Adam had been tied to almost every single memory that had come back to me. And Adam was gone now. But I wasn't about to get into all of that.

"It's pretty random. They kind of flash into my head, like lightning. One second they're gone. And the next second they're back. But each time it's happened, someone has been there with me."

"You've had none when you were focusing alone? When you're actively trying to access those memories, they stay in the dark?"

"Right."

"Well, if what you want to do is to remember, and by the way, in my professional opinion that would be best, I have one question."

"Okay. Shoot."

"Do you think maybe you should stop trying so hard?"

I sat there speechless. Dr. Guest shrugged her shoulders.

"That's so simple," I said.

"It might just work."

"And you get paid *how much* for this?"

Dr. Guest tipped her head back and laughed. I realized that I'd never heard her happy, only concerned, and the change was nice.

"Okay, then." Dr. Guest plopped her pad on the table, the pen scooting across the page of squares. "Here's your homework. You're going to give yourself a break. Just relax and stop focusing so much on the memories. Live your life. Spend time with your friends. Wait and see what happens."

I sat there thinking that her advice could be applied to many areas of my life. The missing memories, obviously. And Adam. Sweet Adam, who had changed so much. Pushing him was the worst idea I had ever had. But Dr. Guest's homework might help me handle my frustration over how to deal with Shannon. I had been unsure how to confront her, trying to come up with some grand plan that would end with her explaining everything in a way that made all the pain disappear and that, at the same time, might bring us all back together again.

Since that would never happen now, I figured I had nothing to lose. I deserved a break. And it just might be my turn to be unpredictable and go a little crazy for once.

17

The Earth Spinning Beneath Me

I stared at the flames of the bonfire, watching them leap and dive in front of me, my fingers wrapped tightly around a bumpy stick as the fire licked the sides of the marshmallow I was roasting. I felt hazy, like I was only half there. It had nothing to do with alcohol—I'd only had a few swigs from Tanna's special Fourth of July mug, just to keep her from asking questions about why I'd been so quiet lately. It had worked. She was sitting next to me on a knotted log, singing along with a bunch of people as Pete played Jason Mraz's "I'm Yours" on his guitar.

It had started thirty-eight days ago, the dreamy fog I'd been swimming through. Since Joey's death, life had been swirling by in swatches of color, waves of sound, thunderous moments of truth. And it was all out of my control. I knew it was up to me to regain some kind of order. But I wasn't sure how. So I kept treading, ever so lightly, through each moment and into the next.

But then the marshmallow fell. Slid right off the end

of that stupid stick. And everything that I'd been trying to hold together leaped right after it, directly into those writhing flames.

"Maggie!" Shannon squealed from a few feet away. "I just told you we're almost out of marshmallows."

I watched the marshmallow bubble and fizz from its place in the ashes, a blue flame melting it into a goopy mess.

"Here." Shannon stepped around the fire and plopped down beside me, holding out the near-empty bag of marshmallows. "*One* more chance."

People were all around, sitting on lawn chairs circling the fire, waiting for the fireworks to start as they roasted their own marshmallows to perfection. A shout came from a cluster of people bunched around the game of beer pong set up on Shannon's back porch. Everyone was at ease with Shannon's parents out of town, savoring the music, the fire, and the summer night.

Everyone except for me. I batted Shannon's hand away, nearly toppling the fresh marshmallow to the ground. "I'm good."

Tanna whipped her head around, her hair flicking me in the face. "What's wrong with you?"

"Whaddo you mean?" I asked, trying to tear my eyes away from the flames.

"You live for s'mores, Maggie. Don't try and tell me nothing's wrong."

"You really need to ask?" I flashed her a warning just-leave-me-alone look. She might have taken the hint. If it wasn't for Shannon.

"Yeah. Something's *definitely* up. I thought it was just me. But then I watched you totally blow Pete off earlier tonight."

"I didn't blow Pete off," I said, trying to keep my voice steady, my eyes away from her face, because I knew very well that I had. I'd been so surprised to see Adam round the corner of Shannon's house, I'd turned away from Pete and practically run. I hadn't seen Adam since the creek, more than a week ago, and I had no idea what I was supposed to say to him. Or anyone else, for that matter.

Pete stopped playing and turned to us, his lips parted like he wanted to say something, but he kept quiet.

"Pete was in the middle of a sentence and you just walked away." Shannon gave me a little snort. I wanted to claw at her perfect little throat. But that image made me think of Joey's lips, his warm breath, his tongue, all tracing their way up to her pretty pink lips. My whole body started to shake with a fresh rush of anger.

"You *have* been acting a little off lately," Tanna said, tipping her head to the side and gazing at me like she was thinking that if she stared long enough maybe the real me would come through.

I rolled my eyes. "You think?" I asked. "Not like there's a reason for me acting differently or anything."

From the corner of my eye, I saw Shannon looking at me with the same intensity. She leaned forward, her hair falling over her shoulder. "Oh. My. God. You remembered, didn't you?"

I looked at her then, the way her eyes had lit up, glinting in the flickering light of the fire.

"You remembered what happened at the top of the cliff." Shannon's eyes locked on mine. "Tell me the truth, Maggie."

Her words made me laugh. It was a sick sound that burst from me before I could contain it. And it brought Adam over from the shadows of the trees, his face creased with concern.

"What's going on?" he asked.

I stood and swiveled around, facing him. "Shannon thinks I remembered something from the cliff top."

Then Shannon stood, shoulders pulled back, chin up, her face a tight mask of anger. "I'm telling you, I've felt it all along. *Something* happened up there."

"What happened between me and Joey at the top of that cliff is none of your business, Shannon."

"The hell it isn't." Shannon looked right at me, her eyes harder than I had ever seen them. Meaner and more accusing than when she called Nick Hadley out for stealing Pete's guitar back in eighth grade. "Why didn't you jump, too?" Shannon asked. "How come it was only him?"

"*I don't remember*," I said, my words shaking with a fresh wave of anger. How could she stand there and accuse me after everything she'd done?

"He was all twisted up, Maggie. Bent backward," Shannon said, her voice dropping. "Like he didn't get the right start. Which makes no sense, because he's jumped that cliff about a thousand times since eighth grade."

"It was an *accident*." Pete shook his head. "He was crazy-stupid sometimes. We all know that. And no matter how much we talk through this, I don't think we're going to get the answers we're after."

"We might." Shannon shrugged, tucking a strand of hair behind her ear and tipping her head my way. "If only she would *remember* something."

"Shannon, that's enough!" Tanna stood and placed a hand on my shoulder. "We're all freaking out here. You can't blame Maggie any more than the rest of us. We were drinking. And Joey? He was the kind of guy who would take a walk in the park and find a way to make it reckless. This whole thing is a terrible tragedy, Shan. But the only person to blame is Joey."

"Guys," Pete said, "Joey would *not* like what's happening right now."

"But why aren't we asking more questions?" Shannon asked. "Why haven't we—"

"What, exactly, are you accusing me of?" I asked, my entire body tingling. I felt disconnected from everything. The scene unfolding in front of me wasn't reality. It couldn't be.

"I think you have a secret—something you don't want *anyone* to know—about what happened up there on the cliff." Shannon's words exploded into the dark night.

"Oh, now here we go. Let's dig in, shall we?" I clapped my hands together and stepped closer to Shannon. "I find it ironic that *you're* accusing *me* of having a secret. You have one of your own, don't you, Shan?"

The anger in Shannon's eyes flared and then flashed into something that looked like fear. "What are you talking about?"

I swiveled, walked around the fire's edge, and yanked Shannon's purse from under her lawn chair. I was pissed at myself for leaving the photo album at home. I'd thought about bringing it but was worried that having it close would make me want to attack Shannon. And earlier, I hadn't been ready to face her. Because facing her meant everything I'd had with Joey would be all the way over. And everything we'd all had together, that would be over, too.

When I turned, Adam was there. "You don't want to do this, Maggie," he said, his voice a shaky whisper.

"Yes," I said, "I do."

"Here?" Adam swept a hand in the air, indicating all the people standing around, clutching beers and staring. "With all these people watching?"

"Why the hell not? They're gonna find out anyway, the way rumors fly in this town. Some of 'em probably already know." I shrugged, turned, and pressed my way back to the fire before I lost my nerve. Shannon's mouth dropped open as I yanked at the zipper of her purse and turned the bag upside down, toppling nearly the entire contents on the grass before my fingers wrapped around her phone. Adam came up from behind and stood at my side. It felt good to have him there, almost normal, but I worried that he'd try to stop me before I was through.

"I was just wondering," I fumbled around, pressing buttons to find the messages, ducking away from Shannon as she leaped toward me, grabbing for her phone.

"Wait," she said. "You have no right—"

"*I* have no right?" I laughed, tipping my head back

toward the heat of the flames. "Now that's funny. Almost as funny as you asking me to tell you the truth."

Pete rushed up from behind me and grabbed my arm. "Guys. Enough, okay?"

"No. I don't think so." I stared at Shannon, not even trying to wiggle loose from Pete's firm grip.

Tanna moved closer, trying to get between Shannon and me. "What the hell is going on here?"

Shannon's eyes flickered between me and Tanna and Pete and Adam.

"What's the matter, Shan? Wondering how much I know? Trying to figure out which parts to reveal?" I stepped toward her. Held the phone in the air between us, the string of text messages a wall that would divide us for the rest of time. "It's over, Shannon. I know everything."

Shannon swiped the phone from my hand and looked at the lines of text. "Fine," she said. "It was me."

"What was you?" Tanna asked. "Somebody tell me what's going on."

"I'd love a clue, too," Pete said, his hand dropping from my arm.

"The night of Dutton's party, when Joey didn't go home, that's because he spent the night with Shannon." I crossed my arms over my chest, looking right at Shannon. I wondered if she'd admit everything. The sick truth is that I almost wanted her to deny it, so I could still hold on to a tiny slice of hope that my Joey was the real Joey.

"What?" Tanna asked.

"Whoa," Pete looked from Shannon to me and back again. "Why didn't you just tell us?"

"Because, Pete," I said, "there was a lot more to it than that."

"Wait." Tanna threw a hand up in the air. "I'm sorry? What the hell?"

"Right. I know!" I giggled, this crazy sound that sparked in the supercharged air. "That's exactly what I was thinking when I found the pictures."

Shannon's entire body stiffened. Then she pulled her shoulders back and looked me right in the eyes. "You saw pictures?"

"Someone left them on my front porch. There were, like, twenty shots perfectly arranged in this cheesy little album. And the pictures, they told the story of a sweet little romance. One that had been going on for a year, if I had to guess."

"Almost." Shannon stared at me, a flicker of nervous excitement in her eyes. "It was *almost* one year."

I stepped forward, my hand screaming to smack her pretty little face. It made me sick, looking at her, thinking of how many years I'd considered her one of my best friends. "You wanted me to find out, didn't you?"

"I left so many clues, you'd have to be blind or stupid not to have—wait a minute. . . ." Shannon looked into the fire, her face glowing in the orange-tinted light, her brain stuttering over some new thought that I wasn't so sure I wanted to hear. "You already knew . . . *before* Memorial Day weekend, didn't you? That's what happened up there?"

"Shannon, let it go," Adam said.

Shannon looked to the ground, her fingers twisting, twisting, twisting a ring on her left hand. Then she looked up at me again. "Joey and I might have had secrets. But yours, it's way worse, isn't it?"

"You were supposed to be one of my best friends," I said, "and this is what I get after finding out you and Joey had been together, hiding some twisted romance for a year?"

Shannon shrugged. "Afraid to be out of the spotlight, Mags? Afraid of what'll happen now that people know he loved me, too?"

"Are you serious? You think that I'm angry because of—"

"I kept it a secret, Maggie, after he was gone. *For you.* I stood there in your shadow and let everyone console you like you were the only one who mattered. So don't try to act like I didn't think about your feelings."

"I'm supposed to feel sorry for *you* now?"

"No," she said, tipping her head to the side. "And you don't have to feel sorry for Joey, either."

"What the hell is that supposed to mean?"

"Remember that night at your house? Before the funeral, when you told Tanna and me how guilty you felt that he was still a virgin? Well . . . ," Shannon said, her lips curling up in a little smile.

That's all it took.

One simple string of words.

Our friendship, the one we'd taken a lifetime to form, it vanished into nothing during the exhalation of a single breath.

"Shannon!" Adam stepped into our circle, placing his hands on my shoulders and squeezing tight. "That is enough!"

"Adam, get the hell off me," I said, trying to pull free

as he twisted me toward him. I jerked sideways, but it did nothing. His grip was solid, and I wasn't getting away.

"Maggie, it's time to leave." Adam's voice was firm, forceful. But there was something else there, too. An undercurrent of fear that swelled into every syllable. Fear that, at first, didn't seem to make any sense at all. Until I realized the one thing that had been missing since I first confronted Shannon. Surprise.

It clicked into place when I looked into his eyes, the echo of his voice tumbling through my mind, crashing through the different levels of my awareness until I understood without question. "Oh, my God," I said. "You and Joey were fighting about *this*, weren't you? You knew everything this whole time?"

"Maggie, you have to let me explain."

I shook my head. "You've had plenty of time to do that, Adam."

"I couldn't just—"

"Adam, I don't want to listen to one thing that you have to say."

And that's when they started. With a triple bang, the first of the fireworks splashed into the sky, painting all of us a sparkling red, white, and blue.

All the energy that had been driving me suddenly drained away. I felt deflated, like someone had sucked the life out of me. And I had to sit down.

Right.

Then.

Right.

There.

I tucked my face into my hands and scrunched my eyes so tight I thought I might blink away the entire world.

But when I opened them, the world was still there.

I knew because of the feet circled around us.

The fireworks' erratic drumbeat in my chest, Adam's hand rubbing my back, his voice whispering in my ear, "Please, just talk to me Maggie. Please listen to what I have to say."

The lip gloss and purple pen and key chain that I'd dumped from Shannon's purse.

And the bracelet. Perched on a little tuft of grass.

The band was a thin leather strap.

I knew without thinking that it had once been tied around Joey's wrist.

Moved with him, sliding up and down with the swing of his arm.

And the three turquoise-colored glass beads strung right in the center.

The sun had once played with those beads, like the flash from the fireworks did now, glistening off their smooth sides, spilling out to tint the world a bright shade of blue.

"Oh, Shannon." I pressed one hand into the cool grass, the earth spinning beneath me, and reached out with the other. "You didn't."

Then I had it. That string of leather, laced between my fingers. Those cool beads flashing in the sparking light. Sending waves of memories through my already tormented mind.

Dash. Crash. Splash.

18
Then Suddenly I Stopped

"We're gonna go on three," Joey said. "You ready?"

I shook my head. "No."

"You trust me?"

I looked at him then, took in his freckled nose, the wisps of damp hair clinging to his forehead, the way his smile always tilted to the left.

I nodded. "I trust you."

He squeezed my hand again. "Everything's gonna be fine."

I ran my thumb up the inside of his wrist, feeling his blood, his life, pulsing through his body.

"One."

The cool shock of those glass beads zapped my skin like I'd been electrocuted.

"Two."

What was it about those beads?

"Three!"

Running.

We were running.

Almost there.

But the thunder of my feet crashed through something in my consciousness.

And I knew.

Those beads, they were Shannon's.

A vision flashed into my mind—the dream catcher her grandmother had given her when she was little, broken, on the floor of her room, Tanna kneeling down, apologizing, while Rihanna's voice filled the air around us. Shannon plucking the beads from the spiraled web, stringing them on a necklace that she would wear only for special occasions.

And another flash—school-enforced, ninth-grade cotillion, when Joey chose Shannon for the final song, a waltz, and I'd been so jealous I thought I might burst. Until Adam stepped up to me, his eyes intense, hand extended, and asked if he could have the honor of one single dance. I'd accepted, trailing through the room with his arms tight around me, but I'd kept track of Joey and Shannon. It was easy, the way those beads caught the light from the chandelier and threw shimmering bubbles all through the room.

Those beads, she thought they were protective. Sacred.

No one was supposed to touch those beads but Shannon. Ever.

Yet there they were, threaded on the leather strap that was tied around my boyfriend's wrist.

My momentum slowed, my arm tugging Joey's back.

His hand held tight. Pulled me on.

We were only a few feet from the edge of the cliff.

And then, in a quick succession of broken images, I remembered. Her barrette in his console, lying there like it had been flung aside in a rushed moment. His shirt balled up on her bedroom floor, and the flimsy excuse she'd given for it being there. The mix CD she burned for him for Christmas that I wasn't supposed to see. The times I'd smelled a hint of her perfume when she was nowhere near us. How their hands always lingered when they passed a bottle we were sharing. How, when we were all together and I was watching Joey, he was usually watching her. And how she was always watching me, a strange flicker of anger in her eyes.

It was like I hit an invisible wall, one that did not exist for Joey.

I had been so close to flying.

Then suddenly—I stopped.

Dug my feet into the dusty ground.

Yanked my hand from his.

And. Refused. To. Go. On.

He kept moving, though, slower, twisting back to face me, a question in his eyes.

"You and Shannon?" I asked breathlessly.

He tried to stop then, waved his arms in the air to catch his balance, the glass beads on the leather string clicking together.

"Mags, let me exp—"

And that's all I got from him. His shoulders pulled him backward. There was too much momentum for him to stop. So he tried to twist forward again, but the movement just tripped him up, angled him for more of a dive than a jump.

The last thing I remember of Joey alive was the fear in his eyes, their electric blue sparking like embers in a raging fire. There was regret there, too.

I understood the fear. He knew. Maybe not that he was going to die. But he knew he was in major trouble. With me. With the ledge. With the water sparkling below him.

But the regret. That's what I'd like to ask him about.

If I had one more moment with Joey, I'd ask what part of it all he regretted most in those last seconds of his life. Was it lying to me? Crushing me into nothing? Or did it have more to do with the part where he'd been caught?

19

Releasing Their Grip

"Ever since I figured out they went behind my back, I've had this sick feeling in my stomach," I said as I weaved my way through the crowd at Gertie's Dairy Farm, a cone with a single scoop of mint chocolate chip in one hand, a wad of napkins in the other. "It's like I'm one second from puking all the time now."

"I still can't believe it," Tanna said from beside me. "Joey and Shannon. It's just *weird*."

"He had to feel awful," Pete said. He was right behind me, his guitar pressed between us as we made our way to the side door of the huge shop, which was packed wall-to-wall with people out for a country drive and afternoon on the farm.

"Not awful enough." I stepped on someone's foot, and when I turned to apologize was elbowed in my side, so I gave up. "And Shannon—keeping everything to herself after he died—she didn't feel a bit of remorse."

Pete pressed his lips together, silent as we separated
196   from the main crowd.

"As twisted as it is, I think she was trying to protect you," Tanna said through a bite of her strawberry ice cream and waffle cone.

"Like Adam?" I asked with a snort. "Don't even get me started on him."

"Maggie," Pete said, "you have to understand—"

"No. I don't. Adam's worse than both of them. At least they had a reason to keep their twisted little secret."

I stopped to toss my gum in the trash can by the door to the side yard, which was peppered with picnic tables and old tractors for kids to climb on. Without thinking, my eyes grazed the corkboard hanging on the wall. It was supposed to hold seven pictures of Gertie's most daring patrons, the ones who had taken on and conquered the Big Dipper Challenge. But now there were only six. In place of the seventh photograph, marking its former existence, was a dark square of corkboard, the edges surrounding it faded by sunlight and age. My feet stopped, shoes planted to the sticky, pink tile floor.

I stood there, staring at the board, trying to remember every detail of that day from the previous summer. How Joey had accepted the challenge on a whim. How he'd let each of us pick two flavors for his ten-dipper sundae. How, when he held his stomach with a pained face, we'd all cheered him on, telling him to keep going.

"Shannon was sitting right next to him," I said, shaking my head.

"Maggie, what are you talking about?" Pete's face creased into that worried-about-Maggie look that was starting to make me feel crazy.

197

"The picture from Joey's Big Dipper Challenge," I said, pointing up at the empty space. "It's gone."

Tanna glanced over my head and sighed. "Wonder who did that?" she said, taking another bite of her ice-cream cone.

"His other girlfriend, maybe?" I asked sarcastically. "She was sitting right next to him that day. I remember her ring, glinting in the sunlight from the front window, as she handed him those tiny plastic cups of water."

Pete pushed the door open and Tanna and I followed him out into the bright light of another humid July day. In an instant, I felt like I'd been sucked away from the present, taken back to so many moments from the past in one burst of thought. I saw him everywhere. Joey feeding the goats a handful of pellets from the dispenser. Joey balancing on the top of the wooden fence to the pigs' pen. Joey leaning up against the silo, standing in the open door to the cow barn, leaping onto a tractor. Joey. Joey. Joey. How could he be everywhere and nowhere at the same time? How long would the realization continue to stab into me? And then, just as quickly, be followed by the slicing thought of Joey and Shannon together?

"Should we sit here?" Tanna asked. "Or do you want to walk out to the trails?"

I was about to say that I wanted to get away from the crowd, to sit in a clearing deep in the woods while Pete played us a few songs, to simply hang out and not talk about all the stuff that hurt so much. But that's when we heard him. I knew we all did, because Pete's and Tanna's eyes looked as sad as I felt.

I looked over Pete's shoulder and found him, Joey's

brother, along with several of his friends, pouring out the side door of Gertie's, ice-cream cones in hand.

"It's Rylan," I said softly. "Just Rylan."

The group walked right past us, over to the main tractor. From the corner of my eye, I saw a few of them climb the large front wheels to sit right on top of the worn tread, while three others fought for the driver's seat and steering wheel. But not Rylan. He'd stopped just a few steps short of Pete and Tanna and me. He was just staring. Like there was something important he wanted to say.

"Ry," I said. "How are you?"

Rylan shrugged and licked the top of his ice cream, moving a few steps closer. "Pretty sucky."

"Yeah," I said. "Me, too."

"We had people in town for the Fourth last weekend, relatives all up in my face. People crying, and sniffling, and snotting. They try to hide it. Take me out to do some random thing, but that only helps for a little while."

"Yeah." I moved my ice-cream cone from one hand to the other, feeling like one taste would make me sick. "Nothing helps for very long, does it?"

Rylan looked at me, his eyes creasing. "You're probably one of the only people who really gets it."

I sighed. "I don't know if that's true."

Rylan's mouth twitched. "I heard about what happened at Shannon's. I don't have a clue what I'm supposed to say." Rylan's eyes flicked to Pete and Tanna, then back to me.

"I don't think there's anything you can say."

"No. Probably not." Rylan shook his head. "He could be a real ass sometimes, that's for sure."

"Yeah," I said. "But the hard part is that he could also be pretty perfect."

Rylan moved closer, his eyes glinting in the sunlight, so much like Joey's that it hurt me in a deep place I hadn't even known existed. "My mom knows, too. She wants to talk to you, Maggie."

I closed my eyes, thinking of Shannon's accusations and how Mrs. Walther would have so many more questions now. "I don't think I'm ready for that yet."

"But you'll call her? When you are ready?"

"Sure," I forced out. "I'll call soon."

"Good," Rylan said. "I'll see you guys later."

I watched as Rylan ran toward his friends and the tractor, taking a giant leap and scrambling up to the top of the right front tire. I looked down, realizing both my hands were empty. My ice-cream cone lay splattered at my feet, a soupy mess. The wind tossed all the napkins I'd yanked from the dispenser, twirling them around in lazy circles.

"Maggie, are you okay?" Tanna asked.

"No," I said, thinking of facing Joey's mother. "What if she has the same questions Shannon does? What if she blames me for something? I don't know if I can—"

"Maggie, stop. Mrs. Walther wouldn't think that way. And Shannon, she doesn't, either. Not really."

"Yeah," Pete said. "Shan's just trying to cope, like we all are, and doing a pretty shitty job at it."

Tanna grabbed my hand then and pulled me away from the crowd, across the field of grazing cows, their crooning twining around the rays of sunlight that pierced the air. Through the back gate with the crooked door that only latched if you made it. Into the woods that stretched for miles and miles and miles, eventually dumping you out on the cliff top where everything had begun.

Or was that where it had ended?

I was no longer sure.

"You have to ignore it," Pete said, his fingers dancing across the guitar resting in his lap.

"Which *it*?" I asked, leaning back against the rough bark of a tree, staring through the clearing and toward the narrow trail nearby. I wanted to run to the end of the world. Jump off. And free-fall for the rest of time.

"The stuff with Joey and Shannon. All the lies. Focusing so much on all that is going to make everything worse."

"You make it sound so easy," I said with a snort.

"I don't mean to be like that," Pete said. "But you have to figure out a way to deal."

"I keep thinking that it couldn't have gone on for too much longer," Tanna said. "With everything you're find-ing out, I think it was about to all blow up in his face. But he died and left it all behind for you to untangle."

"I have to do this right." I clawed at my chest, wanting to rip away the anger. "If I don't, I might never get rid of this feeling."

"It's gonna hurt," Tanna said. "There's no way around it. You gotta find a way to go straight through the pain and get yourself to the other side."

"You sound like my shrink," I said with a chuckle. 201

"She'd totally agree. The thing is, I was starting to handle Joey's death okay. I mean, as okay as I could. But this is way worse, because this kills him in a different way. The Joey I thought I knew, that Joey never existed, did he?"

Pete shrugged. "The Joey you loved, he was *real*, Mags. Don't let his thing with Shannon take that away. You have to figure out how to separate everything if you're gonna make it through this."

"How the hell am I supposed to separate anything at this point?"

"Maybe spend some time remembering special stuff you did, just the two of you." Pete strummed the guitar, spilling a chord out into the rays of sunlight trickling down through the leaves.

"Don't let this new person take his place in your mind, Maggie," Tanna said. "Joey would hate that."

"I keep wondering how he would feel," I said. "Wondering what he would say. You know, if he were here and he could."

"Me, too," Pete said. "And every time I think about him and you, and the whole thing with Shannon, this one song pops into my head."

"Oh, yeah?" I asked.

"Yup. It's kinda cheesy, but I feel like he's sending it to me. Just for you." Another chord poured from the guitar and tripped through the trees. "I can play it if you want."

"Yeah," I said, scooting away from the tree and lying on the grass, looking through the leaves at the too blue sky. "That would be nice."

As soon as Pete started, I knew the song—Nickelback's

"Far Away." My eyes filled with tears as the lyrics streamed into my mind, and I wanted to tell Pete how perfect the song was. But I wasn't so sure I could get the words out. Tears slipped down the sides of my face, and I tried to swipe them away, but they kept coming, so I let them fall.

I felt so sad and alone, even with Tanna lying close by, even as Pete started humming the tune. I wondered if Joey had really loved me, if he missed me from wherever he was. He felt so far away, I held my breath and tried to remember something that would bring him back. Something that would make me feel all the right things instead of everything that was so very wrong.

As Pete hit the chorus and Tanna started singing the words, a ribbon of wind flowed through the treetops, pulling a leaf from its hold on a high branch. The waxy green teardrop tumbled and flipped toward me in slow motion. And that's all it took to bring him back.

My Joey.

We were almost two years in the past, lying on a blanket in the gorge, looking up at the trees, which were dressed in fancy reds, yellows, oranges, and browns. We didn't talk or laugh or even kiss. We just lay there, my head on his chest, looking up-up-up the bodies of all those towering trees. They were almost silent, but when I listened really closely, I could hear them whispering reassurances into the air around us, speaking of trust and daring, of just letting go.

The amazing thing was when they did it, when those leaves simply freed themselves. Joey and I, we just watched as the reds, the yellows, the oranges, and the browns released their grips from the tangled arms of those trees. We watched, and they took flight in a spiraling, swooping ride that left me breathless.

20

Surprises in the Strangest Moments

"Maggie, we called you in today because we'd like to know if you've remembered anything else from the day Joey died." Detective Wallace's mustache twitched around his words. His slender hands were perched on top of the same conference table from that terrible Saturday when I'd lost Joey forever. I wondered how many questions had been hurled across its faux wood surface over the years.

"My client is still in therapy," Mr. Fontane said from his seat beside my father, who had insisted that I sit between him and my mother when we took our places around the table. "She is working with Dr. Guest to recall those lost memories. We have already told you that we'll offer anything of significance as soon as we can."

"Dr. Guest's original reports suggest that Maggie may be suffering from either post-traumatic stress disorder or dissociative amnesia, both of which may leave her unable to access her lost memories. With all due respect, our investigation can't just sit idle, waiting to discover the outcome of her therapy." Detective Meyer pressed his thick lips together.

"We have some new information," Detective Wallace said. "And we'd like to hear Maggie's side of the story."

Not ready to face whatever they were about to throw my way, I tried to sink back into my chair without being obvious. Detective Meyer, however, caught me and stared into my eyes. I tried to hold my head up, but the shaking in my hands had traveled up my arms and taken over most of my body. I felt like I had the shivers, but I was hot and a little sweaty. I looked to my lawyer, trying to focus everything on him, trying to drown out the detectives.

Mr. Fontane clicked his tongue on the top of his mouth. His hair was combed back tightly, stiffened by some kind of product. It looked exactly the same as it had the day Joey died, when I'd met with him for the first time. He'd sat on the recliner in our living room, asking all kinds of questions. Questions that I could not even think about answering, not even now that I did remember.

"What type of new information?" my mother asked from her seat beside me.

"Apparently, there was a party on the Fourth of July during which Maggie and another young woman had a confrontation." The words spilled out of Detective Meyer's mouth in a way that made me sure he had rehearsed them.

"Shannon," I said with a sigh. "She talked to you?" But then I wondered if it had been someone else. Like Joey's parents. That thought brought some of the old panic back, the nervous feeling of guilt that had taken over the day Joey died.

"We can't divulge that information." Detective Meyer sat back in his chair, placing both of his hands on his large belly. "What we can share is that while we had been ready to close the investigation, our final interviews raised some new questions."

I wanted to stand up and scream at the detectives. Scream so loud I melted the skin right off their smug faces, so hard I'd blast Shannon right off of this miserable earth, so long I might be able to bring Joey back so that he would have to face what he'd done.

"We've learned that there may have been some kind of altercation between you and Joey before the accident. The individual we spoke with thinks something may have happened on top of the cliff that caused Joey to fall to his death." Detective Meyer stared at me, waiting for any reaction. "Something between the two of you."

"Did this person tell you anything about that supposed altercation?" Mr. Fontane asked.

Detective Meyer clasped his hands. "We'd like to hear Maggie's side of this story."

I looked at Mr. Fontane, wondering if it was time for me to speak. He stared down at the papers in front of him. "I've advised Maggie not to say anything today. I think it's best to have her therapist's approval before we proceed."

Detective Wallace cleared his throat. "We'd really love to settle this matter."

"So would we," Mr. Fontane replied. "But not at any risk to Maggie's well-being. She has been struggling to deal with the events that occurred on Memorial Day weekend, and Dr. Guest has advised her parents and me that we should not push her for answers."

That part made me feel the most guilty. I hadn't told anyone about the memories that had flooded me on the Fourth of July. As backward as it seemed, Adam was the only person I wanted to talk to about the cliff top. Since he'd been up there with me after everything happened, I felt like he would understand. But I couldn't get past my anger. All I could think was that he'd known everything and kept it from me, and I didn't know if I could ever face him again. So I'd held on to Joey's last moments for an entire week, keeping the secret my own, wondering how, and when, and if I would ever share it with anyone else.

The air-conditioning kicked on with a *whir*, covering my arms in goose bumps.

"You were about to close the investigation?" my father asked. "Does that mean you have the results from the autopsy?"

Detective Meyer nodded his head. "We do."

"And if you were going to close the investigation, that means that you didn't find anything to indicate foul play." Mr. Fontane looked from one detective to the other.

"That is correct," Detective Wallace said with a curt nod.

"To be frank," Mr. Fontane said, sweeping his papers into a stack and leaning down for the leather briefcase that was propped against the leg of his chair, "I'm not exactly sure what we're doing here."

"I'm with you," my father said, his words tight. "You're keeping an investigation open because a girl who could be holding some kind of grudge against my daughter made some wild accusation?"

"We have not revealed the source of our informa—"

"We all know who it was." My father's voice rang through the room, shaking with anger. I was surprised by his insistence, by the way his hands had balled into fists, by how red his neck and cheeks had turned. But most surprising of all was how my mother just sat there, doing nothing to get him under control. Not that he lost it often, but when he came close, she was always the first person to rein him in. "If you look into Shannon's relationship with Joey, you'll find that she's not exactly known for her honesty."

"Regardless, *suspicion* is a strong word, Mr. Reynolds," Detective Meyer said, his belly rising with the intake of one deep breath.

"We'd simply like to know if there was a conflict between Maggie and Joey on the day of his death." Detective Wallace looked right at me.

"I've read the transcript from the first time you questioned my client," Mr. Fontane said. "She's already stated that Joey did not seem to be in conflict with anyone on the day of his death. Beyond that, she has complied with every one of your instructions." Mr. Fontane stood then, his briefcase thwapping against his leg.

"She most certainly has," my mother said, standing and placing a hand on my back.

"Then," Mr. Fontane said with a shrug, "we're done here."

"Understood," Detective Wallace said.

"Yes," said Detective Meyer. "And it should also be understood that this investigation will remain open until we have all the answers we need."

My father stood and pulled my chair back. I got to my shaky feet, wondering if my facial expression or body language or the fear radiating from me would tip anyone off. If it was obvious that I had remembered exactly what had happened up there on the cliff top and was keeping it a secret in spite of everyone wanting the truth.

Because if they could read me, I was screwed. Joey's death may have been a terrible accident, but it was one that I had caused. All because I'd trusted him too much and was too afraid of letting go.

"I made your favorite," my mother said from her perch on the side of my bed. "Pot roast, carrots, potatoes . . ."

I flipped over to face her, yanking my earbuds from my ears. "I'm not hungry."

My father stepped in from the hall, his hands tucked into the front pockets of his jeans. "You have to eat, hon."

"Not now." I couldn't imagine eating. I was sure anything I swallowed would come right back up. "My stomach," I said, curling into a ball, "it's not right."

My mother sighed. "I can only guess why. That Shannon. What was she thinking?"

I heard the anger in my mother's voice. Solid, reckless rage. I loved her for it.

"We can't worry about it right now," my father said, leaning against the footboard of my bed.

"What are you going to do, sweetie?" my mother asked, her fingers swiping loose strands of hair from my face.

"Sleep," I said, my voice croaking the word out.

"You're sure you don't want anything to eat?" my mother asked. She smiled then. "I have peanut butter pie. What about a totally unconventional peanut butter pie dinner? I can come up and eat some with you. Right here in bed." She smoothed her hand across the patches of the quilt pulled over my legs, taking them in, seeming to wish for the simplicity of the past, thinking of all those years, of the love, and pain, and acceptance those tiny little squares represented.

I sat forward, hating the way her eyes lit up at the prospect of me accepting something as insignificant as a piece of pie. Had the riptide of this whole thing pulled me that far off course?

"I'm going to be okay, Mom." I patted her hand, realizing how similar our long, slender fingers were, and even the shapes of our fingernails.

My mother sucked in a breath and tears filled her eyes. "I know you are, Maggie."

"You're one tough cookie," my father said, tipping back on the heels of his shoes.

My mother and I looked at him, then each other, and laughed.

"What?" he asked, throwing his hands in the air. "You are."

His confusion made us laugh even harder. The doubled-over, almost-pee-your-pants kind of laughter that sometimes surprises you in the strangest of moments.

It felt good, breaking open like that. And it lightened the room by about a thousand pounds. I leaned back against the headboard, propping a pillow behind me, and asked my father to go get us all a slice of pie.

When he left the room, I pointed toward the end of my bed. "Tell me about that red one. The shiny patch of satin near my right foot." I wiggled my toes, bouncing the section of quilt up and down so she'd know where to look.

My mother's fingers found the square of fabric, traced its perfectly stitched border. "That one," she said, "is from the dress I wore to my senior prom."

"No way," I said, sliding farther under the covers for her story. "You have to tell me all about it."

Her voice swirled around me then, a cocoon that gave me a much-needed reprieve from everything that had happened since Memorial Day weekend. We spent the rest of the evening together, hanging out in my room, my mother telling my father and me the stories behind each and every one of those worn swatches of fabric. As I listened, losing myself in each little tale, I realized that the quilt would not have been the same, not nearly as beautiful, without the sadness. The robin's egg blue patch from a baby blanket that had belonged to my uncle who died when he was two, the purple satin ribbon found after a tornado destroyed my grandparents' first home, the black silk from the dress my grandma wore to her father's funeral—those slices of life, they were just as important as the rest.

21

Independence Day

It was Friday the thirteenth, and I knew a party was going on somewhere nearby. Tanna had invited me, but I'd said there was no way I was going to chance running into Shannon, who had never missed a party in her life. I'd watched a cheesy slasher movie on the couch before coming up to my room and falling into bed, my iPod in hand, ready to scroll through my music to find something that wouldn't remind me of Joey. Or Shannon. Or Adam, for that matter. After an hour, I yanked the buds from my ears, frustrated that the people I was trying to forget seemed to be attached to every song in my playlist.

It was a little after eleven when the text came through.

U know I luv u, right?

Yes, I replied. *I always feel the luv, T.*

Good. Bc I'm on my way over.

No, I texted back. *I'm gng 2 bed.*

U can't, came the reply. *Adam's in trouble.*

I sat up, staring at the words, dread spreading from my chest to the rest of my body until I felt numb all over.

I'll b there in 5, Tanna added. *B ready.*

Tanna's car pulled into my driveway and squealed to a stop. The windows were down, and the first thing I noticed was the lack of music pouring from the radio. Then I saw Shannon sitting in the passenger seat, her eyes locked on mine, her face void of expression.

"What the hell is she doing here?" I asked.

"Dude," Pete said from the backseat, "we don't have time for this. Just get in the car."

"No! I'm not going anywhere with her."

"What part of '*Adam's in trouble*' did you not understand?" Tanna asked, leaning through the open driver's side window. "Get in the freaking car, Maggie. We have to find him."

I crossed my arms over my chest and took a step back. "He's been missing in one way or another since Memorial Day weekend. What's so different about tonight?"

"His mom called." Shannon said. "She's worried because he had some appointment today that he missed. And then he never went home."

"He's not answering any of her texts or calls." Tanna ran her hands along the steering wheel nervously. "And even with everything we've seen, she said he hasn't totally ignored her until tonight."

"Blowing us off is one thing," I said, my level of anxiety

exploding. "But it isn't like him to make his mom worry. Especially after Joey."

"So, you coming or not?" Pete asked, leaning between the front seats like he wanted to drag me into the car. "'Cuz we gotta *move*, Mags."

"Where have you checked?" I walked around the front of the car to the passenger-side door as Shannon swung it open.

"Nowhere yet," Tanna said. "We came for you first. We were thinking we could drive around to see if we can find his car."

"If he doesn't want to be found, he won't leave his car out in the open," I said.

Shannon stumbled out of the car, her shoes clicking on the driveway, and crossed her arms over her chest. The thick scent of liquor surrounded her, and I looked down to her feet, knowing that this was not the time to confront her about what she'd told the police. But, God, I was dying to. Instead, I pulled Shannon's seat forward, lifting one foot so I could climb into the back, and my thoughts returned to Adam.

"He's hiding, so we have to think." I pictured him, then, the moonlight streaking his hair, his feet dangling over the rushing water. Heard his voice trailing through my mind: One *of my hideouts.* "Wait! The creek. He's got to be at the creek." I shoved away from the car and ran around the side of my house, through my backyard, and toward the trail that led to the woods.

The wind picked up, rushing through the trees above, whispering in a frantic way that made me feel like we had to hurry, like Adam needed help and we were running out of time.

As we raced deeper into the woods, I heard someone stumble behind me. Then Shannon said, "Shit, Maggie, slow down already."

That only made me go faster. When we stepped from the line of trees to the edge of the creek, I fully expected to see Adam sitting there on the rock, right where I'd found him three weeks earlier, his green eyes flashing silver in the moonlight. But there was no moon—it had hidden behind a thick batch of storm clouds that raced overhead. And there was no Adam, either. The rock sat in a deep shadow, flat and cold, and so very alone.

"He's not here." The words exploded out of me, my breathing tight and quick as I turned in a circle, hoping he'd appear in the time it took me to spin back toward his rock. But it didn't work. "I thought for sure he'd be here."

The creek rushed by, curling in little waves, competing with the sound of the wind.

"We need a plan," Shannon said. "We can't just run around like freaks all night."

"I'm not a freak," I said, turning to face her.

"I didn't say *you* were a freak, Maggie. Just that—"

"Whatever," I said, rolling my eyes. "What you think hardly matters to me anymore, anyway."

"Well, the police seem to feel differently," Shannon said. "Thankfully, they—"

"Holy shit!" Pete shouted, jumping between us. "It's Friday the thirteenth."

216   "As if you didn't already know that?" Tanna asked.

"Yeah, but, it's Friday, *July thirteenth*." Pete's eyes were frantic, hardly focused, and I wasn't sure if he was really seeing any of us.

"Right," Shannon said. "And that matters because . . . ?"

The wind tossed Pete's dreads up in the air. "It's Independence Day."

"Oh, my God," Tanna said, her voice competing with the wind. "The cliff. There was something about a tradition with you guys, right?"

"July thirteenth is the day we took our first jump. And we swore we'd do it again, every year on July thirteenth. But it has to be a night jump to count."

"Oh, God," Shannon said. "That means we have to—"

"I can't go there." I backed toward the trail, shaking my head.

Tanna grabbed my hand and stopped me. "You have to, Mags. He's been so upset, pulling away from us, all because he's been keeping this secret from *you*. You need to hear him out, to listen to his reasons."

"Tanna, I—"

"Maggie, you're the only one who's gonna get through to him right now."

"Bro!" Pete shouted up the side of the cliff, his hands cupped around his mouth to be sure his words reached Adam. "What are you doing up there?"

We were standing in front of the Jumping Hole, the wind twisting around our bodies, all of us looking up.

Adam was at the top, standing at the edge of the cliff, dark clouds rushing across the sky behind him.

"This isn't funny," Shannon yelled.

"I'm not trying to be funny," Adam shouted. He swayed a little, back and forth. "I'm celebrating my freedom!"

"He's been drinking," I said. "What the hell are we supposed to do?"

"This isn't a *we* thing," Tanna said, turning and looking at me. "This has to be you."

"You're kidding, right?"

Tanna bit her lip. Shook her head.

"You have to go up there and get him," Tanna said. "He's not going to listen to any of us. He's hating himself right now because of what happened with you."

I thought of all the messages he'd left, all the texts I'd ignored since the Fourth of July. Adam had been trying to apologize and I'd shut him out. But then I looked to the ground, the wind tossing my hair wild, my eyes tripping over to the spot where Joey had been lying the last time I was here.

"This isn't my fault!" I screamed. "I didn't do *one thing* to cause this! Why the hell should I have to go up there?" Then the tears came, falling from my eyes faster than I could swipe them away. I did not want to be crying, but everything inside me had surged forward and pushed its way out.

"Stop being so self-absorbed," Shannon said with a sneer. "Adam is up there and he needs you. Just like you needed him the day Joey died."

"Self-absorbed?" I shouted. "Did you really just call me—"

"Yes!" The wind carried Shannon's word and whipped it into the night. "You've been at the center of this thing from the beginning, Maggie. With your boyfriend gone and your memory gone, everyone's been tripping over themselves to make sure you're okay. I've had to watch from the sidelines. No one knew how I really felt. And now that I have a chance to share how this has affected me, all I get is people talking behind my back about what a bitch I am. What I did might not have been right, but I loved him, too, Maggie."

"You expect me to care?" I asked. "After you ran to the police and tried to convince them that I had something to do with Joey's death? Give me a fucking break, Shannon."

"Guys!" Pete yelled, his face twisted with irritation. "This is *not* the time."

"Where'd he go?" Tanna asked, her head tipped back, her words frantic. "Where's Adam?"

"All clear?" The voice trickled down to us, the meaning of the words slamming into me so hard they almost knocked me down.

"No!" we all shouted at once. The thunder of our voices crashing through the gorge brought Adam back to the edge of the cliff.

"It's as clear as ever," Adam shouted, waving a finger side to side. "It's not nice to lie, you guys. You should've learned that much by now."

"Stay there," I shouted. "I'm coming up."

"Maggie," Adam called. "I have to do this."

"Just give me five minutes," I shouted. "Please."

Adam swayed with a gust of wind. Then he sat down, dangling his legs over the side of the cliff. I was relieved and scared half to death. Adam was safe for now, but I had to get myself up to that cliff top and talk him down. All without allowing my memories to pull me into a total panic.

The creek was so swollen, the Jumping Rocks were almost underwater, and I had to hop carefully from one to the next as I made my way across the bridge they created.

When I got to the other side, the trail was dark.

Black-hole dark.

"You can do this." I whispered the words to myself over and over, the reassurance stringing out into the night, trailing up into the sky to be carried away by all those rushing clouds.

Branches cracked under my feet with almost every step. Leaves rushed and spiraled in the harsh wind, restless for a place to hide. As I hiked up the trail, I wondered if the wind was trying to keep me away. It seemed angry. Strong.

But tonight, I was stronger.

"You can do this."

The cadence of the repetition calmed me. Kept my mind from what I was about to do. If I thought about it, I might stop and turn around. And that was not an option.

Adam needed me.

I stumbled on the root of a tree. Fell to the ground, my

hands catching me as a loud grunt escaped my lips. My fingers dug into the moist bed of the trail, the trail I had last traveled with Joey. No, wait. That had been Adam. I couldn't believe how mixed up everything still was, even with all my memories in place.

I smelled rain, a metallic scent that told me the clouds were about to break open. I needed to hurry.

I pushed myself from the ground, finding my footing. My hands shook as I dusted them off. My legs wobbled, threatening to buckle. I wanted to stop. But I couldn't. I *had* to do this.

My hands reached out for every tree that I passed.

A thin tree with smooth, silky bark.

A gnarled tree, bumpy like an old man.

An oak. Giant. Revered.

And all of them dancing, their limbs whirling in the air, their leaves hushing and shushing my mind.

The wind picked up, twirling my hair into the sky. I grabbed the mass of waves, twisting them into a bun, my fingers sinking into the silky strands as I took my last steps toward the cliff.

He was there. Sitting alone. Just looking down.

I walked to him, past the shrine of dead flowers that our classmates had brought here after Joey's death, trying not to think about why they were there, snapping in the wind, and put a hand on his shoulder. "Adam, what's this about?"

"I don't know anymore, Maggie." He ducked his head. Shook it from side to side.

I wanted to sit next to him, knew it was the best thing

221

to get him out of this place, but I couldn't. So I just stood there, my hair whipping into my eyes, wondering what the hell I was supposed to say.

"It's my fault," Adam said. "Everything with Joey."

I sighed. Squeezed his shoulder and let my hand fall away. "Nothing's your fault, Adam."

"It is, though. If I'd just told you, none of us would have been here. You and Joey wouldn't have been on top of this stupid cliff, and he wouldn't have fallen." Adam's words slurred together. He was in worse shape than I'd thought.

"Adam, there's stuff you don't know. Stuff that makes this my fault, too."

Adam looked back at me, his eyes tight. "What are you talking about?"

I shook my head. "I can't," I said, my words choking in my throat. I did everything I could to look into Adam's eyes and at nothing else. Not the treetops that had surrounded Joey and me right before the beads made me understand his betrayal. Not the feeling of my hand yanking out of his. Not the way his eyes had swelled with fear, and sadness, and regret as he lost his balance and pitched over the edge of the cliff.

"Maybe you can't tell me," Adam said. "But I should, shouldn't I? Just like you wanted me to the day of the funeral. When you tried to make that deal where we'd share everything. I need to tell you. All the shit I knew, and how I found out. You deserve to know, Mags."

I stepped back as he spoke. One step. Two. Three. Because I didn't want to know. All the details would slice me open again, and I couldn't face that. Especially not standing up there on that cliff top.

"No!" I said. "I'm not ready. Not for all of that."

Adam closed his eyes, burying his face in his hands. "I can't seem to get anything right anymore."

"You can," I said. "I want to know. Just not right now. Right now, all I want is for you to stand up and walk down the trail with me. I want you safe, Adam."

"But I won't be safe, Maggie. I'm all messed up inside. Besides, tonight I'm supposed to jump. It was an oath sacred to our friendship." He smiled then, this thin smile that was so sad.

"Adam, you can honor Joey in a different way. Please. Don't jump off this cliff and leave me standing here all by myself. I can't face that again."

It was then that it seemed to register in Adam's brain. Where he was. Where he'd brought me. The recognition passed across his face like one of the bloated clouds that raced above us.

"Oh, Jesus, Maggie, I—"

"Adam, it's okay. Please, just—"

"So sorry. I can't believe I'm such an asshole." Adam twisted sideways, placing a hand on the dusty ground. He pulled his legs up and swung them around, skidding his feet along the little biting rocks that carpeted the earth.

And then he stood.

Way too fast with all the alcohol, and wind, and emotion.

He started to sway, his arms shooting from his sides, sweeping up and then down.

I didn't have time to think.

All I could do in the moment was react.

My feet rushed me forward—one step, two, three—and my arms snapped forward, my fingers gripping the front of his shirt. I yanked him into me before I took one single breath. Wrapped my arms around his waist as he fell against my body, his breath hot on my neck.

"Please don't hate me, Maggie." Adam's voice cut out on him, turning into a croaky cry. His shoulders shook, and he tipped his forehead onto mine, his eyes squeezed tight. As he slipped his face into the curve of my neck, I sucked in deep, even breaths to keep myself under control.

Then the rain started, cool drops that made my skin tingle. I focused on each one, hoping they had the power to wash away everything, so we could just start over again.

I smoothed the loose strands of Adam's hair and he started to quiet down. His tears spilled down my skin, under the neck of my shirt, and into the places that only Joey had explored.

Adam pulled away slowly, looking right in my eyes. He cupped my face in his hands and shook his head. "I am so sorry, Maggie. For everything."

I nodded, feeling his fingers brush the skin of my jawline. He hesitated for a moment, his eyes focused on mine.

"I know you are." I sucked in a shaky breath, holding on to him tight. I wouldn't let him go until we were standing at the bottom of that trail, until we'd crossed over the Jumping Rocks and were safely on the other side. "And I could never hate you."

"You know we have to talk, right?" Adam raised his

eyebrows. The rain was falling harder now, dripping down his face and onto the tangle of our arms and hands.

I nodded.

"I'm here. When you're ready, you just let me know."

I nodded again, because I wasn't sure if I could speak.

Adam ran a hand through his hair, pulling his bangs out of his eyes, and looked around, raindrops falling from his chin and nose. It's like he was looking for Joey, like he wanted to say one last good-bye. But we'd lost that chance. That moment had passed.

I wrapped an arm around Adam's waist and tugged him toward the trailhead. He slung his arm over my shoulders, moving slowly, stumbling every few steps. His body was warm, solid, and so very alive. And I'd never been so thankful for anything in my entire life.

22

All the Pieces

"It's okay, Maggie," Dr. Guest said in her most gentle tone. "You can tell me."

So I did. I let it all surge from deep within my chest, an angry storm breaking me open.

Dr. Guest sat still, taking it all in without moving one single inch.

When I was finished, I looked down, afraid of the disappointment I might see in her eyes.

"You're blaming yourself, aren't you?" Dr. Guest asked. "For what happened on Memorial Day weekend?"

"How can I not? He died because of me."

"Joey's death was a terrible accident, Maggie. It, however, was not your fault." Dr. Guest raised her eyebrows, waiting for her words to sink in.

"If I'd just kept running. If I'd jumped with him. If—"

"You can 'if' yourself to death—*if* you want—but I'd advise against it." Dr. Guest crossed one leg over the other and leaned back in her chair. "You have enough to sort through without simultaneously playing out every other possible outcome."

I nodded. Because I'd already thought of that. "What am I supposed to do now?"

"What do you think?"

"I hate when you do that," I said. "Turn a question back on me."

"Usually you have the right answers. I just encourage you to dig deep enough to reach them."

"I'm thinking I'll just ignore it. Pretend I still forget for the rest of my life. I haven't told anyone yet." I looked at her, narrowing my eyes. "Everything I say to you is confidential, right? So it's, like, against the law for you to tell?"

Dr. Guest smiled. "What do you suspect might happen if you try to ignore all of this? It's pretty big."

"Ignoring it might make it go away."

"What if it makes everything worse?"

I clasped my hands together, folding them in my lap. I thought of walking into school in the fall for my senior year with the gray cloud of Joey's death, all his lies, and Shannon's betrayal hanging over me. I knew it would suffocate me. Eventually.

"Maybe you should just tell everyone the truth." Dr. Guest threw her hands up in the air, like she'd just had some epiphany.

"The truth?" I asked. "As in, the *whole* truth?"

Dr. Guest shrugged. "It's just an idea. Sounds like there are already an awful lot of secrets."

"If I let everything out, if everyone knows the truth, people will hate me. It's *my* fault Joey died."

"Some people might be angry. But when they hear the entire story, I suspect most people will support you. And that support might just help you learn to stop blaming yourself, Maggie."

I shook my head. "You don't understand. Joey was this legend at our school. Bigger than all of us put together. Everyone knew him. And everyone loved him."

"Do you still wonder if anyone *really* knew him?"

I thought about that. Just a few months ago I thought I'd known Joey. All of him. But I'd been wrong. "Maybe Shannon did," I said, the words twisting around my heart and pulling tight.

Dr. Guest nodded her head, a serious look crossing over her face. "Then maybe she's the best place to start."

"Shannon?" I shook my head. "No way. I can't ever speak to her again."

"It might be worth a shot, Maggie. You still have your senior year to get through. She's been like a sister to you almost your entire life."

"No. I can't."

"Think about it," Dr. Guest said. "I'm not suggesting that you try to rebuild your entire friendship. Just that you go to her and deal with the feelings that are making things so messy right now. Show her that you can face everything that's happened. Free yourself from this prison Joey and Shannon built around you."

I imagined myself walking into Shannon's bedroom. Sitting on her bed, where I'd slept so many nights. Where Joey may have slept . . . with her. I visualized opening my mouth to speak. But all I could hear was me telling her off.

"What about Adam?" Dr. Guest asked. "Have you talked to him since the night you found him on the cliff top?"

I shook my head.

"That's another thing you'll have to figure out."

"This is one hot mess."

Dr. Guest chuckled. "It might feel like that, Maggie. But actually, you're doing very well—making monumental progress with your memories and ability to share. If you think about how you want it all to look in the end, if you take the right steps to get there, you might actually find yourself feeling happy again."

I snorted. "Doubtful."

"You have all the pieces in your hands," Dr. Guest said. "You just have to decide where to put them."

I thought about that, playing with the idea throughout the rest of our session. I knew I had all the pieces, I could feel the different textures sliding in my hands. The problem was, most of them were jagged-edged, slicing into me when I tried to figure out how to order them, how to stitch them back together. So I envisioned throwing them all up in the air, running, and hiding from them forever.

23

The Very Center of Our Lives

I wasn't going to do it.

Not.

Ever.

But when I left Dr. Guest's office, new thoughts started pinging around in my head. If I spilled all my secrets, maybe Shannon would do the same. If I told her the one thing she needed to know, maybe she would tell me the thousand things I wished I could avoid. As much as I didn't want to hear about her and Joey, I knew ignoring them wasn't going to fix anything. Tanna had been right: the only way to the other side of this was straight through. And as much as I hated to admit it, I needed Shannon to help me get there.

It took a few days, thinking of how I would say all that I needed to. How I'd escape if she leaped toward me, assaulting me with the blame that I was trying to erase from my mind. Thinking of the insults I'd hurl if she attacked me with those words.

But even with two days of planning, I hadn't been able to prepare myself for her reaction when I shared the story of what had actually happened on top of the cliff.

Instead of rage-inspired threats, Shannon crumpled into a ball on the floor of her bedroom and stared at a patch of sunny carpet near her right foot.

"Shannon," I said. "Are you okay?"

I looked down at her, the way she'd started rocking slowly back and forth, her arms wrapped around her knees.

"It was the bracelet?" Shannon asked. "That's what did it?"

I nodded. "That's when everything clicked into place."

"It worked, then." Shannon looked up at me with tears dripping from eyes. "I *wanted* you to know."

I sat next to Shannon on the floor, leaning against her bed, oddly numb in the moment of my big revelation.

"I left clues all over the place," she said. "My barrette. His shirt. A pack of gum. My favorite pen. But you never figured it out. I had to think of something that I *knew* would work."

"Your random clues were kind of normal, though. We all have each other's stuff, Shan." I looked at the carpet, wanting to close my eyes and squeeze everything out. But I couldn't. Not anymore. "Why didn't you just tell me?"

"Joey would have killed me. He wanted it to end naturally between the two of you so it wouldn't seem so wrong when we ended up together. But then he kept dragging things out. Playing these games that made me think he was about to end it with you. Then we'd all hang out, and I'd hear some story about the great night the two of you'd had alone. I was so confused. And getting really angry."

"When did Adam find out?" I asked.

Shannon's eyes squinted tight. "I honestly don't know. I think he suspected for a while, but he wasn't sure. Joey kept stuff from me because he didn't want me to freak— and I *was* freaked about what we were doing to you—but I just had all these feelings and I didn't know what to do with . . . "

"Spare me, okay?" I said.

"Right." Shannon swiped her palm across her cheeks, wiping away her tears. "I know Adam was pissed, Maggie, and he wanted Joey to tell you. Then Adam threatened to tell you himself, the night of Dutton's party."

"So that's what the fight was about."

"Yeah." Shannon sighed. "I wanted you to know, too. But I didn't know how to tell you. I wasn't sure I could— so I just didn't."

"I don't understand the bracelet," I said. "If you knew Joey was going to tell me, why give him that bracelet to wear? It's like a slap in my face."

Shannon squeezed her eyes. Tight. "He broke up with me. The night of Dutton's party." Shannon sucked in a deep breath. "He said he'd been wrong. That he loved you, not me. He wanted it to be over between us before he told you."

"That's . . . crazy."

"I know." Shannon laughed, this choked sound that resembled a cry. "Joey was crazy. But I was, too. Crazy pissed off. He'd always been yours, and I thought it was time he was mine. So when he dropped me off the second time that morning, I told him to wait. That if it was over,

I wanted him to have something to remember me by. I ran inside and grabbed my necklace and tied it around his wrist before he left."

"Because you knew I'd figure everything out if I saw those beads."

Shannon nodded. "I'm sorry. I was just so . . . wrecked."

"And you wanted me to be wrecked, too?"

"Kind of. God, I know that's awful, but I couldn't believe, after all that time, he was choosing you. That I was so monumentally stupid to think he ever would have chosen me."

"It wasn't so stupid. You two had been together for a long time."

"Yeah. In hiding. Because I wasn't good enough to be seen with in public."

"I'm sure it wasn't about that," I said. "Sounds like, in his twisted mind, he just wanted to keep us all together."

"And look how it ended. A complete disaster."

I could not believe that we were sitting there just talking this whole thing over like it was nothing. But then I thought of all the emotion that had swelled up since Joey's death, the explosive night on the Fourth of July, how long we had been friends, and this moment somehow seemed to fit. It was the only way for us both to get what we needed.

"Mrs. Walther reamed me when she found out." Shannon caved into herself as she said the words.

"You talked to Joey's mom?"

"Yeah. After the Fourth of July, when Rylan told her about me and Joey, she called and asked me to go over there. She'd heard about me going to the cops, and let's just say she was more than a little pissed."

"I was, too," I said, thankful that Mrs. Walther wasn't angry at me, knowing that I needed to go see her soon. "Still am."

"I'm sorry," Shannon said. "I shouldn't have gone to the police. It was stupid, but I know everything now, so I can fix it."

"I don't know if it can be fixed," I said. But I didn't mean the stuff with the cops. I meant everything else—Joey's death, my memories of him, the lifelong friendship we all had shared. The important stuff had been ruined, and there was no way to get it back.

"Will we ever be friends again?" Shannon asked.

I shrugged. Thinking about it made me feel *all* that I had lost. Joey's death should have brought the five of us closer together. Instead, it had ripped us apart.

"When I tied my necklace around Joey's wrist, making it into a bracelet for him, I didn't care about my friendship with you. I just wanted to shove the big secret out in the open. But now I hate myself for being so focused on the wrong thing. And I can see that this mess isn't just Joey's. It's mine, too. Problem is, I'm the only one left to clean it up."

"We can help each other, you know," I said.

"How?" Shannon asked.

"The cops. They still have lots of questions. I could maybe go to the station with you to tell them everything."

"The part where everything is *my* fault, you mean?" Shannon dipped her face into her knees. "If I hadn't given him that stupid bracelet, he'd be alive right now, Maggie."

"Shannon," I said, "I've been blaming myself in one way

or another since the day he died. But the thing is, while we all played a part in what happened, it was an accident."

Shannon looked up at me, tears streaking her face. "Yeah," she said. "Maybe you're right."

"Does that mean you'll go talk to the detectives with me?"

I stood then, holding my hand out for Shannon to grab. She looked at me, her cheeks glistening with fresh tears, and grabbed on tight, letting me pull her up.

"Here," I said, shoving my hand into the pocket of my shorts and pulling Joey's bracelet out into the rays of sunlight streaming through Shannon's bedroom windows. The light winked off the smooth surface of the glass beads, splashing brilliant blue puddles into the space between us. "This is yours."

"Maggie, I—"

"Shannon. I don't want it."

Shannon didn't say another word as she tugged the leather strap from my fingers and turned, walking to her dresser, arm outstretched toward the velvet-lined box that had housed those turquoise beads for so many years. When she pulled the top off, I saw it buried snuggly within. The picture that had been taken the previous summer at Gertie's Dairy Farm. The one where all of us had gathered around Joey, arms raised in celebration after he conquered the Ten-Dipper Challenge, mouths spread in wide, carefree smiles. I realized as I stood there in the middle of Shannon's sunny bedroom that Joey had positioned himself right where he thought he belonged—in the very center of all of our lives.

24

Back to the Beginning

"I like this hiding spot so much better than the other one," I said as I stepped from the trail, walking to the rock where Adam was standing and looking down at the water. I kicked my shoes off and sat back on the cool rock beneath us, listening to the trickle of the creek as the sun slowly dipped behind the thick of trees just off to our west.

Adam sat next to me, the movement stirring the air enough that I smelled him—the soapy, sweaty, summery scent making my vision swim. Adam tilted his head toward me, his face glowing in the sugary pink tint of the sky.

"I figured you'd never speak to me again," Adam said. "After the cliff top last weekend."

"You're lucky," I said.

"I know I am."

We were silent for a while, the good kind of silent you can only have with a close friend. I sat there next to him, breathing in the scent of the summer, listening to the call of the crickets, a lazy breeze blowing through my hair.

"You ready to tell me what happened at Shannon's house on the Fourth of July?" Adam asked, breaking the stillness that had settled around us.

I shrugged. "You were there."

"I'm not talking about the stuff I could see. You went into that strange daze again, just like the day of Joey's accident. Totally freaked me out. I'd appreciate it if you'd stop doing that." He poked me in the side with his elbow.

"Yeah. I'll try." I shoved my hand into the pocket of my shorts, strangely missing the feel of those three slippery beads.

"You remembered, didn't you?"

I nodded. And then I told Adam everything. He was silent as my words twined around us, soft and bruised, fading into the now velvety blue sky.

"There were so many clues, Adam. I can't believe I didn't see it before." I turned toward him as his arm wrapped around my side, pressed my face into his neck, feeling the steady throb of his pulse against my whispering lips. "I was so stupid."

"No, Mags. Our lives, our stuff, it's all mixed together. Seeing Shannon's things in his truck or his things in her room shouldn't have made you suspect a thing. With the six of us, that's just how it goes." He held me then. Let me cry. When I stopped, he sighed, but he didn't say one word.

"I just want to find an end," I said. "I want to reach the point where I know everything and can be okay with it all."

"You want me to tell you what I know?" Adam asked.

I didn't. Oh, God, I didn't. But I had to hear it. "Yes. I'm ready."

"You're sure?"

I tried not to be angry that he knew all the things I didn't. That he hadn't told me. I couldn't let the emotions get in the way. "I'm sure."

"Okay." Adam took a deep breath. "If I do this, I have to do it right," he said. "Which means we're going all the way back to the beginning."

Adam looked right at me, took in a deep breath, and then the words poured from him, trailing into what was left of the dim light. "Remember your first night with Joey?"

"The meteor shower?" I smiled. "Of course I remember. He drove me out into the field outside town, and that's where everything started." I pulled my knees to my chest and wrapped my arms around my legs, looking at a twisted pattern of rocks that was scattered across the trail. My movements felt disconnected from reality. Like this wasn't really happening, me sitting there, about to learn everything Adam already knew.

"He took that from *me*, Maggie. All of it. I'd told him that I liked you, that I wanted to ask you out. Told him my exact plan—the meteor shower, the crickets, the music. And he couldn't handle the thought."

"You . . . Wait, that was all you?" I thought of the stars shooting across the sky, how Joey and I had lazed under them for hours, kissing, and touching, and giggling. I'd felt so special, thinking that Joey had wanted to share that magic with me. With *just me*, and no one else. But now my favorite memory of Joey was tainted. Adam would forever be in that field with us, standing off to the side, and I would never be able to push him away. "You're the one who told him about the meteor shower?"

"And the donuts. He never would have known what you liked and didn't like. He didn't pay enough attention. And he didn't have the patience to find a field with the least light pollution and best angle of the sky. *I'm* the one who spent weeks scoping out the best spot in town." Adam sighed. "I don't want to hurt you any more, but I have to tell you the whole truth. He challenged me. Said if I didn't ask you out by the Friday before the meteor shower, he'd do it for me. I had no idea he meant he'd steal the whole plan. And you."

. My hands were shaking. My teeth chattering. My entire body started to shiver.

"When I missed his deadline, I didn't think anything of his stupid challenge. I figured I still had plenty of time before the meteor shower to work up my courage."

"But Joey asked me out, instead." I clasped my hands together to stop the shaking. "I remember it was exactly one week before the meteor shower, because I spent every moment of every day wondering what his surprise could be."

"That's about right."

"Why didn't you tell me?" I closed my eyes, not wanting to look into his.

"You were so excited, Maggie. I didn't want to ruin that. And I figured he'd screw it up in a few months, so I just let it go."

"But then we kept going, Joey and me."

"Right. You seemed happy with him. And I knew the way I felt about you didn't matter anymore. You didn't feel the same. At least not about me."

Even with all the ways I'd learned to distrust Joey in the weeks that had passed since his death, even knowing that the last year of our relationship had been filled with secrets, I'd never considered that our very first moment had been a lie as well.

"Joey never gave me the chance to find out how I might feel about you," I said. "But I don't get what that stuff from way back in the beginning has to do with anything now."

"Even back then," Adam looked down at his hands, "I was trying to protect you from finding out who he really was."

I couldn't speak. The emotion riding the wave of his words scared me. Deep-down, can't-move kind of scared.

"It killed me, watching him with you, knowing that it should have been me. But there was nothing I could do."

"Until you found out about Joey and Shannon." The irritation that he'd known so much and never shared it with me rippled through my words. "You could have done something then."

"Yes. I could have."

"When did you figure it out?"

"Homecoming." Adam looked toward the creek. "I didn't know for sure, but that's when I started to suspect."

"The night his grandpa had the stroke?" I was confused, my brain trying to catch up with the information Adam had just given me. "Joey left town to go to the hospital that night, how could—"

"He wasn't at his grandparents', Mags."

Those words hit me hard, and I almost told him to stop. Because I knew from just that one sentence it had been worse than I had ever imagined.

"Where was he?"

"Home."

"The whole night?"

"I'm not sure. I saw the lights on when I drove past after the dance. Haley and I were on our way to the homecoming after party."

"I remember the party," I said. "Tanna tried to get me to go."

Everything in me flipped over everything else, twisted and writhed. One tangled mess. And then it all tripped over to Shannon. Where had she been? At the dance, with everyone else. She'd tried to get me to go, too. Called and called and called. Then, at about ten, Tanna stopped by before everyone in her group headed to the after party, asking if I wanted to join. She'd told me that Shannon was sick and had gone home.

"Shannon skipped that party," I said. "And she *never* misses a party. She was at Joey's, wasn't she?"

Adam nodded. "I saw her car parked against the house in the shadows where the driveway curves toward the backyard. I could hardly make it out, but I was sure it was hers."

"Is that when you called me?"

Adam nodded. "I'd been worried about you all night.

When I heard that Joey had gone out of town—before I knew he *lied* about going out of town—I wanted to leave the dance to get you. But Tanna said I shouldn't. She said I couldn't afford to piss Haley off on our first date. Not that it mattered, since we never had a second date, but whatever."

"Then when you saw Shannon's car . . ."

"I didn't know what to think. I wondered if you were with them. If you'd at least heard from him."

"But I hadn't."

"That's when I knew something was going on."

"So what'd you do?" I asked. "Did you call him that night?"

"I did. After I dropped Haley off at the party. And again on my way to your house with the pizza. But he didn't answer."

"So you came to my house to cover for him?" I asked, anger blazing through my chest. "To keep me from finding out?"

Adam closed his eyes. "Don't compare me to him. I did it because I didn't want you to be hurt. And because I didn't know exactly what was going on."

"But you figured it out." I was quiet. Waiting. "Didn't you?"

"He didn't answer any of my calls the next morning, either. So I went to his house and when I confronted him, Joey admitted that she'd spent the night there. That he never went to the hospital." Adam sighed and ran a hand through his hair. "He told me it was one time. That they'd kissed, nothing else. He said she just showed up at his house, drunk and crying about some shit with her parents, and as he was trying to calm her down, it happened. He also said they'd talked, and that it would never happen again."

I balled my hands into fists, wishing I had something to hit. "Why didn't you tell me then?" My voice was shaky and taut with anger. "Some stupid guy code?"

Adam looked at me. "It wasn't like that, Maggie."

"So what happened next? I know there's more."

"I thought that was the end of it." Adam took a deep breath. "Until the day of your ACT."

"That day in Bradyville? Joey said he was grounded. That's why he couldn't—"

"He was with Shannon."

"When he was supposed to be picking me up? He left me stranded so he could have a morning playdate with her?" My words echoed through the trees, angry and bursting with pain. I tried to stand up, but Adam stopped me with one hand on my knee.

"He told me she was upset about the kiss, that she felt guilty and wanted to tell you." Adam squeezed my knee. "I honestly thought it ended the night of homecoming. You have to believe me."

"Well, we know from those pictures that it was going on pretty steadily for most of the year," I said.

"The pictures," Adam said.

"You left them, didn't you? On my doorstep."

"Shannon was supposed to tell you after the funeral, but she didn't. And then you found those text messages. I had to do something. So I went to the Walthers' saying

I needed some CD Joey had borrowed, and I searched his room for evidence. I didn't think I'd find anything quite so extensive, and I knew it would be hard for you to see the album Shannon made for him, but it was the only thing I could figure out."

"I don't understand why you didn't just tell me," I said.

"I didn't want to be a part of it, Mags."

"Adam, you already were."

"But to be the one to tell you? To be the one to take all of your memories and trash them? I didn't want you to remember that every time you looked at me."

I sighed. Gazed into the shadows that had overtaken the ground. "What happened the day of the ACT?"

"You can't hate me for this, Maggie. I did the best I could." Adam's voice shook with each word. "The day of your ACT, Joey was flipping his shit when he called and asked me to pick you up. His voice was all shaky, like he could hardly breathe."

"Of course he was freaking out. He didn't want her to tell me anything."

"Obviously, I told him I thought she was right. That's when the tension started between Joey and me."

I looked down then. At the way Adam's hand on my knee felt so normal that I almost didn't know it was there. Realized he'd scooted all the way up against me, his chest pressed against my side so hard I could feel his heart beating against my arm. Felt the way my hand itched to tuck his hair away from his face so I could see his eyes without their curtain.

"What'd he say?"

"He said nothing was going on, kept insisting it was just the one kiss the night of homecoming."

"You're kidding me."

"I believed him, Maggie." Adam looked right at me. "Until I saw them together the night of Dutton's party. Behind the garage. Kissing."

Adam's hand squeezed tighter. I wanted to say something, but I couldn't. The image of Joey and Shannon making out when I was right there, just around the corner, made me feel like throwing up.

"I confronted them," Adam said, "and Shannon ran away. That's when I told Joey he had to tell you. That if he didn't come clean, I was going to tell you myself."

"So that's what the phone call was about? The big argument the night of Dutton's party?"

"He'd texted me that he needed one more day. So I called him to say that he had until we left the Jumping Hole on Saturday, and not one minute more."

I buried my face in my hands. "He was pissed?"

"So pissed, Maggie. Like, I'm-going-to-rip-you-into-small-pieces pissed. He didn't appreciate me telling him what to do. Said I had no right to butt in. That he had it under control."

"Oh, my God." The gorge. Adam was going to tell me after the gorge. And the accident, it kept everything buried deep. I went back to that cliff top. To Joey's smiling face. I heard his words ringing through my head.

You trust me?

"He didn't want anyone to tell me," I said. "He knew it would destroy everything."

"I told him then that he had to be the one to tell you. I knew you'd hate him, both of them, after everything. But if they came clean on their own, I thought that there might be a better chance of you forgiving them. I didn't want you to lose everything. I never thought all of this would happen. And when Joey died, I was torn. I thought it might be best if you never learned the truth. Then Shannon, she expected me to keep their secret, to say that Joey had been at my house the night of Dutton's party. . . . But I couldn't. I thought if I told one truth, all the others would just follow, that Shannon would have to tell you."

"I don't even know what to say." My mind was like a thrashing whirlpool, churning each thought into the next before I could process anything.

"He never deserved you, Maggie. It was always supposed to be me."

I buried my face in my hands, stretching my legs out on the rock, swaying with the breeze. "Adam," I said, looking at him. "Nothing between us can ever be the—"

"Please don't say that." Adam's eyes were intense, glinting in the moonlight. Staring right into me. Those eyes. They were safe. As safe as Joey was dangerous. Everything about Adam was safe.

Adam tipped his head to the side. "I love you, Maggie. Always have. And I'm not going to apologize for doing what I thought was best for you." His voice was this raspy whisper that made my breath catch in my throat.

Adam grabbed both of my hands then. Squeezed tight. That's when everything fell away. It was just us. Sitting there together. The cliff top, the pain, the lies—

everything—suddenly seemed a thousand miles behind us.

As Adam and I sat on that patch of cool rock, barely breathing, our hands tucked between our chests, I wanted to kiss him. Wanted him to kiss me.

It was this perfect moment of clarity. And I felt things. Things I'd never felt before. Things that didn't make sense. Until you flipped them over and they started to make the most sense of all.

But then I thought of Joey. Standing on Dutton's deck. Looking out at Adam and me dancing. The surprise and fear and anger splashed across his face making me feel as if he hadn't really been watching us in the yard that night, but that he'd somehow flashed forward to this moment. Seen us sitting under the rushing leaves of the thick-barked trees, wanting to kiss each other and never wanting to stop.

That's when it hit me—the understanding that I wasn't much better than Joey.

I pushed him away then.

Adam.

Not Joey.

I felt like I had that part all mixed up.

But there was too much swirling around in my mind. I felt as if I might just explode.

"I'm sorry," I said in two breathless huffs as I scrambled to my feet, my fingers groping a tree trunk for balance, clawing at the rough patches of bark.

Adam shook his head. Ran a hand through his hair. "Maggie. You have nothing to be sorry about—"

"Adam"—I held a shaking hand in the air between

us—"God, Adam, I don't even know what I'm doing any-more."

"You'll figure it out." Adam looked up at me with a sad smile. "You always do."

I stumbled back, trying to get some distance between us. I was practically drowning in the waves of need and fear and hope crashing between us.

"Look. I just need some time. This is . . . *crazy*."

"Maggie. I understand." Adam's voice was steady. He hadn't moved from his spot on the ground. "I do. And I don't have any expectations, okay? No pressure. I just needed you to know how I feel."

I wanted to go home. To the only real safety the world had left to offer. I wanted to hide away in my bed, under the quilt my grandmother had made. I wanted to bury myself under the cover of all those years and erase every-thing that had happened.

But I couldn't.

I had to face this.

There really was no other option.

25

Spinning Through the Stars

"Thanks, Rylan," I said from the driver's seat of Joey's truck. I turned the key and the engine roared to life with a familiar sound that caused my chest to ache from missing him. It was strange, the things that brought the pain and loss rushing back to me. I was never ready to face the feelings. Not even now, a full two months after his death. "I owe you one."

"Thank you, Maggie. For telling me everything that happened the day he died." Rylan swiped his knuckles across his swollen eyes.

"I'm sorry," I said.

"At least it makes some sense now." Rylan pinched his lips together. "You'll come to the house? Tell my parents everything?"

I nodded. "Tomorrow," I said. "I promise I'll call and plan a time to visit."

"It'll be hard for them," Rylan said. "But good at the same time." He looked over his shoulder at the car parked one space away from Joey's truck, the one where three of his friends had been waiting patiently while I spilled everything I knew, then turned back to me. "You'll have it here in the morning? Because if I don't have Joey's truck parked in the driveway by the time my parents wake up—"

"I'll have it here just after sunrise," I said. "It'll be in this exact same spot." I put the truck in reverse then, backed out of the parking space, and watched as Rylan hopped into the backseat of his best friend's car.

He didn't watch as I pulled around the side of Bozie's Donuts. Didn't see as I flicked on the turn signal and headed out onto Main Street, the bright lights of the restaurants I passed screaming into the dark night sky (Ha Ha Pizza, Ye Olde Trail Tavern, Carol's Kitchen). I was finally alone.

I sucked in deep breaths as I drove, Joey's scent so strong, even after all these weeks, that I practically tasted him. It was starting to get to me, what I was about to do, and tears burned my eyes. I'd spent so many weeks submerged in my anger, I wasn't familiar with the jagged edge of my pain. But tonight was about facing everything, no matter how difficult it might be.

I flipped on the radio and was shocked to hear the Dave Matthews Band. Dave's voice rippled from the speakers, filling the emptiness surrounding me. The stereo was set to CD mode, and I wondered if this song, *our* song, was one of the last Joey heard the day that he died. I felt like I was hearing the words for the first time, the line about disappearing and being gone, the other about the moon being the only one to follow.

I looked at the moon as I turned onto Blue Springs Road, moving farther from the center of town, the lights, the people, and wondered if Joey could still bathe in its light. I hoped so. He had always loved the night.

When I got to the field, I slowed the truck, flicked on the blinker, and almost drove past. It felt wrong somehow. Being there. All alone.

But it was the only way.

So I turned in, bumping along the uneven ground beneath the tires as Joey's key chain clanged against the dash, and steered myself to the center of the empty field.

"Okay, Joey," I said into the silent, too-still cab of the truck. "It's you and me. Let's do this."

I shoved the driver's side door open and reached behind me for all the things I would need. Yanked them free. Heaved them over the side of the truck's bed. And climbed in the back.

I made myself a little bed using Joey's inflatable camping mattress and the quilt I'd pulled off my bed, then I lay back, looking up at the sky.

"You here, Joey? Because I have some things to say to you."

The only response was a chorus of crickets. But that was okay. Easier, even, than if he'd still been alive and I had to face him—his eyes and his smile and the whisper of his touch—with all of this for real.

"You crushed me, Joey." I took a deep breath. Swiped at the tears that had begun to fall. "You crushed me into a million pieces. First by dying. Then with all of your lies. I feel like I don't even know who you were anymore."

A batch of clouds floated across the deep blue-black sky, glowing from the backlight of the moon. I wanted a message, something I could be sure about. But I couldn't read anything in their shapes or outlines.

"I know everything now. All of your secrets."

I closed my eyes.

"I know you're not a bad person, Joey. You must have been very confused. But the thing is, none of this was fair to me. And I hate that a part of me hates you now. That you'll never be back to help me see you as something new. I just hope that one day I'll be able to forget this messed-up side of you that lied, and lied, and lied."

An owl called out to the night from the top branches of a nearby tree. I wondered if somehow it was Joey, trying to ease my pain.

"Hopefully one of these days, I'll see past all that. Get back to the memories of before, when things were right and it really was just you and me. Back when I was stupid enough to think it would be forever."

I sat up then. Reached into the bag of Bozie's Donuts and pulled out a devil's food.

"Shannon told me that you made a decision the night of Dutton's party. That you'd decided to drop the whole thing with her. That you'd chosen me."

I took a big bite out of the donut and concentrated on the burst of flavor in my mouth. Perfectly chocolate. And then I was ready.

"Joey, I need to tell you one thing. I don't choose you. Not anymore. And if you'd lived . . . if you'd been around long enough to play it all out, I'd have told you the same thing. I do *not* choose you."

I listened, waiting for a twirling ribbon of warm summer

air to bring me a whisper. An apology. Some kind of understanding.

But still, there was nothing.

"It's over, Joey," I said. "I'm letting you go."

I lay back again, wiping the crumbs off my hands, remembering the taste of our first kiss. I played it back then. All the moments that made up our friendship and love and commitment. The way he had made me believe things were. And the way they were in reality.

I spent the entire night there in that field, lying in Joey's truck, my grandmother's quilt tucked around me. I dozed off a few times, but for the most part I simply let myself feel everything I'd been avoiding for weeks. Let it wash over me and take me where I needed to go.

I thought about Adam, too. Couldn't help it. He was there in the field, laced into all the memories in a whole new way.

I missed them.

Both of them.

Joey.

And Adam.

The thing was, while I missed Joey with a sadness so heavy its weight practically pressed me against the ground, Adam was the one I longed to see. It was Adam's voice I wanted to hear. His hands I was dying to touch.

But that part was crazy. Intense. And more than a little wrong.

So I pushed it away as I watched the moon cross from one side of the sky to the other and lost myself wondering if Joey was somewhere up there, spinning through the stars.

26

All Tied Up

Meet me @ the creek? I typed into the keypad on my phone.

My stomach was all tied up. But I did it anyway. I hit Send.

I chewed on the nail of my right thumb, waiting.

I was worried I'd get nothing.

But then I did.

Ur ready?

I took a deep breath.

Yes.

It had been almost a week since Adam confessed everything. A lot had happened in that time, and I felt proud that I'd faced all of it on my own. I wished that it could go back to being simple between us, and that I could just spill it all out to him—my talk with Shannon, how she's still hanging on to Joey like he's coming back to her, our talk with the police, the relief I felt over their appreciation at our honesty, how the case was officially closed. But nothing would ever be simple between Adam and me, not ever again.

I stared at my phone, waiting for his response, panic flashing through me that I had waited too long.

But then my phone chimed, and his reply appeared.

B there in a few.

My entire body sighed with relief.

"I'll be back in a while," I said over my shoulder, hopping up from the couch in our living room, where my parents were watching a movie I'd chosen but couldn't get into.

"Where are you going?" my mother asked from her perch on the couch, a cup of iced tea in her hand.

"The creek," I said. "Just to . . . hang out."

"You look like you're up to something," she said, her eyes crinkling with a question. "Your cheeks are all red."

I waved a hand in the air as I walked past her, toward the sliding glass door that led to our back deck. "Nothing to worry about," I said. "I'm just sick of sitting around here."

"Good." My mother sat forward, placing her glass on the coffee table.

"Very good." My father held a hand up in the air as I passed him, and I swatted it in a high five. "Stay out past your curfew or something. You deserve it."

"Noah!" my mother said, her voice high, but full of humor. "I don't know if that's the best idea."

"The girl needs to have some fun." My father looked up at me, his eyes sparkling with the fire of some explosion on the television, and winked. "But be safe."

"Yeah," I whispered as I slid open the door and stepped out into the darkness of the night, hoping I hadn't just made the biggest mistake of my life.

When my feet hit the dirt path at the edge of our yard, I started to doubt myself. There was nothing safe about what I was planning to do.

Above, leaves fluttered in the moonlight, and I wondered if their whispers were meant for me, if they were imprinted with a code that I needed to decipher. Some kind of important message that would help me get this right.

I focused, listening to their rippling cross over my head, hearing one word in the muggy wind.

Hurry.

Hurry.

Hurry.

I picked up the pace then, as that word echoed through my head. Hoped that I hadn't run out of time. I had to get it right. This last thing. I couldn't lose him, too. And there was only one way to protect what was left between us.

My arms pumped against my sides, helping me gain even more speed. The thick air rushed at me, pulling my hair over my shoulders, whipping it into the silver light of the moon. I wanted to be there, couldn't move fast enough. Each second felt like forever.

But of course, when I turned that last bend and saw him sitting there, I almost stopped and ran back the other way.

Because there was no way to be sure which was the right choice to make.

But I had to trust myself.

There was no one else.

Adam turned as I kicked off my shoes. "Hey," he said.

"Hey." I folded my legs beneath me and took my place next to him on our rock.

"Didn't know if you'd ever call," he said with a half smile, "after everything I told you."

"Yeah," I said. "I needed to work some things out."

"Right," Adam said, turning his face to the rushing water of the creek.

"It was all pretty messy," I said.

Adam nodded.

"And I've been pretty pissed."

"You have a lot to be pissed about."

"I'm talking specifically about the parts that had to do with you."

Adam clutched his hands together in his lap. "Do you need me to apologize again?"

"No. I know you're sorry."

Adam didn't look at me. "I am."

"And I know that you were trying to protect me."

"I was."

"I'm ready to thank you for that part," I said. "For trying to keep me safe. And putting me first." I took a deep breath, noticing the air shift around me. I actually felt lighter.

He looked down then, nodded as though he understood something I hadn't even said, that shaggy blond hair obscuring my view of his eyes. Eyes I suddenly wanted to see more than anything.

"Maggie." Adam sighed. Bit at his lip. "I just want you to trust me again. I hope you can remember, even with everything, that you know me."

"I thought I knew Joey. . . ." My voice trailed off as soon

as his name hit the air between us. The single word soured things. Made Adam's face go hard.

"Don't compare me to him. Not ever." Adam held his hands out in the air like he was about to touch me. I wanted him to. So crazy bad. But he didn't. Instead, he used them to push himself to his feet and turn away from me, toward the water.

"I'm still trying to figure out what I'm supposed to believe. How much I can even trust myself."

"Let me help you, Maggie." Adam turned back toward me, into the moonlight. He hadn't shaved in a few days, and I wanted to rub my hand along the stubble on his cheek. To feel the warmth of his skin. But his words, they rushed me, flipping everything over one final time.

"I have wanted you as long as I can remember," he said. "And it's killed me, knowing what a screwup he was, knowing that you deserved so much better than his lies. But I've sat by and watched. And I've waited. Because I didn't want to be the one to take him away from you."

"Adam, I—"

"And now, when I finally have a chance, they've ruined it."

I looked into Adam's eyes. And I knew. Without a doubt. He was telling me the truth. The feelings between us, they were real. As suddenly as I realized that, it hit me that the most important parts of what I had with Joey were in my own mind. I'd built him up to be something he never really was. I'd kept the truth from myself, and that's why it all hurt so much when it came crashing down on me.

Adam chuckled. "Maggie. Just get it over with," he said.

"It's nice and all, this little blow-off speech, but it's killing me. I know I screwed up. And that you'll never feel for me the way that I feel for you."

"Adam, I—"

Adam interrupted with a deep sigh. "Just please tell me you'll still be my friend. I can't lose you all the way. Not now . . . not ever."

"Are you done yet?" I asked.

Adam nodded.

"Good." I stood up and stepped away from him. Pulled my hair from my face and looked right into his eyes. "Because it's my turn to talk."

Adam sighed.

"I've had all this crazy stuff swirling through my head lately. About Joey. And Shannon. All the memories and guilt that came rushing at me when I found that bracelet." I watched the way Adam's gaze had shifted down to my hands. Felt that he wanted to touch me. "But all the stuff with you, it's been there, too. Not just how you feel—have felt for so long—but how you make me feel."

Adam looked up at me then, his eyes flashing the brightest green.

I had to force myself to go on, to crash through the fear that was nearly suffocating me. "I've tried to shove it all down, but the parts with you, they bubble their way to the surface in the strangest ways. How, at the craziest moments, I just want to feel your hand on mine, or hear your voice whispering in my ear, or feel the tickle of your laughter against my cheek."

Adam smiled. Ducked his head.

Some of that fear melted away.

"I've been trying to sift through all the reasons we shouldn't try this, weighing them against all the reasons that we should."

"Yeah?" Adam asked, his voice hoarse.

I nodded. "There are about a zillion things going against us."

"True." Adam held a hand out to me.

"And we shouldn't." I reached out and placed my hand in his. So sad when I thought about everything that had led to this moment.

"Probably not." Adam squeezed my hand and then let me go.

I stepped toward him, wishing I could cut a swatch of the cool, silky rock beneath my feet, wishing I could use it as the first patch of fabric in the quilt that would make up the rest of my life.

"But when I think about it really hard, when I push everything else away, I realize that I don't care." I grabbed both of his hands. "I don't care one single bit about any of it. I just care about you."

Adam raised his eyebrows, his eyes widening. "Wait. What are you—"

"I'm saying I'm ready. I am *so* ready. To try this thing with you. It's going to have to be slow, right? And I'm pretty sure that I'll have some total freak-out moments along the way. But I can't seem to get you out of my mind. And if you feel the same way, doesn't that mean we should just . . ."

"Give it a chance."

"Something like that," I said, laughter curling over my words.

"You're sure? You're ready?"

I nodded. "I feel like I shouldn't be. Not so soon after my relationship with Joey. But there were so many lies. I needed to come to terms with it all before I could move on."

"And you have? I don't want to rush you."

"You're not rushing me," I said. "I can't wait. Not one more minute."

Adam ran his thumb along my forehead, slowly pulling back my bangs.

"Can I show you something, Maggie?" Adam's eyes lifted, his hands hovered in the air just under my chin.

I nodded. I hoped. But I didn't know.

We stepped closer then, our faces tilting together, closing out the rest of the world.

And this time, this moment, I got everything right.

So very right.

acknowledgments

The overall concept of this book was inspired by several people I've known who moved on before their time should have been up. In their honor, I want to acknowledge everyone who has lost a life too soon, and all of those who were left behind.

Writing a book is an incredible process that comes with many highs and lows. It's also something that I couldn't do on my own, and I'm grateful to have many people to thank for their support.

To Amy Eckenrode, who gave me excellent feedback on police procedure. Also to my team of medical advisors, Tim Beach, Jim Loki, Dr. Tim Schoonover, and Dr. Debra Sowald. Any mistakes in these areas of the book are mine and mine alone.

To Jason Behm for sharing his knowledge of all things motorcycle, and for finding me one that needed a key. And to his lovely wife, Lori, for always being there and knowing the perfect thing to say. (It's time to celebrate, right?)

To Melanie Singleton, one of the only people I know who reads as much as I do, for always being there to brainstorm ideas, for your interest in my stories and characters (I know they keep you up for some late-late nights), and for always giving me incredible feedback.

To Jenny Cooper, for being one of my first readers and my number one musical advisor. Love all of our brainstormy dinners. Those SHS yearbookers rock, too!

To my very first reader, Janet Irvin, who plows through early chapters that should never see the light of day, for your skillful story problem-solving abilities, unwavering support, and for always giving me encouragement to keep going when I need it most.

To Katrina Kittle and Sharon Short, two very talented authors who have become like family over the course of writing this book. I am so lucky to have you to share with and seek advisement when it comes to . . . well, *everything*.

To the remainder of my friends (who are like family) and my family (who are like friends) for always being there.

To all of the supporters who enjoyed *The Tension of Opposites*—your feedback keeps me going when I need motivation. Also to the Class of 2K10 and the Tenners, two groups of awesomely supportive authors—I am proud to be part of your lives.

To Jay Asher, my very first blurber, for a talk in the park, a salted caramel hot chocolate, and all of that lovely praise.

To Regina Griffin, Katie Halata, Mary Albi, and everyone else at Egmont USA for everything that you do. Especially to Alison Weiss, whose phenomenal feedback, guidance, and support helped me wrangle the earliest draft of this book into something I am proud of.

To my mom and dad for always nurturing my love of books. It's because of you that the first glimmer of this dream to become a published author came to life in my mind.

To my children, for your love and for always believing in me. Nothing beats having you in my life.

To Eric, my husband and best friend, you have this crazy way of getting better with each passing moment. Thanks for supporting this dream of mine. For so many reasons, I couldn't be happier.

To my kick-ass agent, Alyssa Eisner Henkin, for always being there, for always inspiring, and for always pushing me to do my best.

Thanks to all of you for believing in me, and for helping me believe in myself. Much love.